The Misadventures of Salem Jack & Finnigan Reeves

Gold Fever

By William Harmening

The Misadventures of Salem Jack & Finnigan Reeves

ISBN: 1500704768

ISBN-13: 978-1500704766

Cover Artwork & Book Design by Allie Daigle

For Zoe and Zander

CONTENTS

1

THE MAP

"I'll bet you this penny," said Jack, as he pulled the shiny copper from his pocket. His eyes sparkled with a certain pride as he displayed the glistening coin in the bright sunlight. He was certain the incentive would overtake his best friend's ambivalence toward the challenge. Besides, on such a hot afternoon, Jack knew the cool current of the river would be far too inviting for Finney to shrug off the challenge.

"So where'd you get that?" asked Finney, trying his hardest to feign a lack of interest. He knew it was a rare occasion for Jack to have money of his own earning. When he did, it was usually just a memory within minutes of its acquisition, just long enough for Jack to trek his way to the Lincoln-Berry store for a colorful candy stick. Like most young boys in a frontier village, Jack saw little sense in saving the spoils of any particular endeavor for any length of time. In his mind money was made for one purpose, and that was to spend as quickly as possible.

"I won it fair'n square!" answered Jack, jutting his chest outward in a lofty sort of stance. "Abe bet this morning the Colonel would plum wear me out before I could catch him with my bare hands."

"You mean that old rooster of Mr. Rutledge's?" Finney hesitated to accept such a grand explanation. He figured it to be some knavish scheme that brought the penny into Jack's possession. After all, catching an obstinate old rooster, especially one not particularly keen on the idea of being caught, was not an easy endeavor.

"Sure enough," answered Jack. "The old bird got me tired as a catfish on a trotline!"

"So how'd you catch him then?"

"You won't believe it! We ran in circles till we couldn't run another step, and when we both keeled over, well, I fell right on top of him!" A smile etched across Jack's freckled face at the thought of his triumph over the Colonel. It had been a much-deserved victory; running down and catching the stubborn old bird. It was the type of sport Jack lived for.

Finney offered a skeptical sort of look as he kicked off his boots and prepared to race Jack across the narrow river to the granddaddy willow tree on the other side. "Yeah, well you won't be so lucky this time! Besides, anyone can catch an old rooster." As Finney discounted Jack's impressive feat, inside he felt a bit of jealously at not being able to boast of a like accomplishment.

"We'll see who the lucky one is," answered Jack, as they lined up at the river's edge. "First one to touch that big limb hanging in the water will be declared the winner." Quickly he returned the shiny penny to a secure fold in the pocket of his pantaloons. Since he seldom wore shoes—weather permitting—Jack had only to sling his straw hat to a spot in the mud next to Finney's boots to ready himself.

"Ready when you are!" yelled Finney. He was confident he could take Jack in the short dash across the river. Being nearly a head taller, Finney could usually get the best of him in a competition requiring the use of his long arms or legs. Quietly he surveyed the water in front of him to chart the quickest route to the finish line. It was just enough hesitation to lose any advantage his superior size provided. The tips of Jack's hands had already parted water when the sound of his hurried "GO!" startled Finney into diving head first into the muddy Sangamon. Up and down the embankment, birds and critters of all sizes scampered to places of safety at the sound of the loud splash. The sound of the commotion echoed its way up the steep bluff toward the log cabins that lined both sides of the village's main road.

"You cheated!" yelled Finney with his first breath, his arms and legs splashing about in the water. Between his wild strokes he coughed to free the mouthful of slimy river water Jack's dishonest method had caused him to gulp in. Truly, he should have expected nothing less. Jack's ability to sucker even those with a keen eye to his scheming ways was well known throughout the village. Whether at Clary's Saloon tempting those confident in their perceptive abilities with his peanut in the shell trick, or perhaps laying in wait at the Lincoln-Berry Store for anyone willing to bet a cup of sweet sassafras against his ability to stand on his head longer than they could hold their breath, Jack was always at the ready to exploit a situation in order to reap some financial gain. Those who knew him best were almost always on their guard never to enter into any such arrangement, lest their hard earned money find its way from their pocket to his. More than once the village constable—and in a few instances even Reverend Cartwright—had lectured Jack about his behavior, thought to fall a bit short of the moral character expected of a boy Jack's age. The lectures had little impact. He just became more astute at hiding his activities from those critical of his knack for turning a coin. In a frontier village of the day, where money to a young boy was as rare as a clean pair of pantaloons, such a talent indeed was a valuable asset.

Half the river's width ahead, Jack busied himself looking back and laughing at the sight of Finney hurrying to catch him. As if to rub salt in the wound, Jack rolled onto his back and began swimming with a lazy sort of backstroke, all the while poking fun at his opponent's attempt to regain a steady course in the water. By now, Finney had cleared his lungs of the murky water and was kicking feverishly to propel himself forward. His anger was evident and only hindered his efforts to regain a smooth and steady stroke.

Now one thing can be said of young boys; they seem to come into the world with a sort of built-in desire to outwit other young boys at every opportunity. The problem though lies in the fact that at times their desire for such battle is so great that the young combatants lose sight of the battlefield. Jack had become so humored at Finney angrily chasing him in the muddy current that he failed to catch sight of a large piece of driftwood that had floated directly into his path. "Hey, wait a minute!" he yelled, as the large branch brought him to a dead stop. To worsen matters, one of its snake-like tentacles had become hopelessly entangled in his shirt. Now it was Jack who fought to regain a steady stroke. The more he flung his arms to and fro, the more tangled his shirt became. Any effort to quickly free himself was easily defeated by the water-logged branch.

The disruption was enough to allow Finney to easily overtake him. "I'll be waiting for you!" Now it was Finney who laughed and rolled onto his back for a lazy backstroke while Jack struggled to free himself from the tangled limb. The victory was sweet. Even the taste of the muddy river water now seemed unusually pleasant. And what better way to defeat a would-be scoundrel, such as Jack was in this instance, than to watch him ensnared by the trappings of his own scheme. A perfect sort of justice, Finney reasoned.

By the time Jack finally pulled himself from the river, his muddied and stretched shirt tangled about him, he could hardly bear the thought of handing over his hard-earned penny to Finney. After all, real money of any denomination was simply not something easy to come by. He searched his thoughts for a way out of his predicament, but no ideas came presently to mind.

"I believe you owe me something?" said Finney, with a devious sort of grin. His victory truly had a sweetness about it, given Jack's attempt to win in the manner he did. With his hand outstretched, Finney had little concern for Jack's downtrodden demeanor, which he quickly surmised to be another ploy. His only thought at the present was acquiring a sweet licorice stick at Abe's store.

"I don't suppose in all fairness, with that driftwood and all, we could race back to the other side before declaring a winner?" Jack cast his eyes downward like a scolded puppy. With the most pitiful look his imagination could conjure up, he decided to play to Finney's sense of fairness, a tactic he had successfully employed many times before against his friend. Of course, if the need did arise, it certainly wasn't beneath him to resort to common begging to keep hold of his precious currency.

Finney recognized the look on Jack's face and its intended purpose. He knew it to be a look Jack routinely used with masterful perfection; one that had the power to secure a piece of apple pie before it even cooled. This time however, the drama was for naught. Finney's smile made it apparent to Jack that his method wasn't working.

"You supposed right," smirked Finney, with his wet hand outstretched. "Now hand it over!"

"Well it sure ain't fair! Ever since the Talisman made it through they've been talking about dredging this river. Now it done cost me the only penny in my pocket!" Jack removed the coin from his pantaloons and tossed it abruptly through the air to Finney's waiting grasp. Quickly, he turned about, unable to stand the sight of his opponent reveling in his victory.

"Ah, quit your complaining." Finney inspected his prize in the usual manner by placing it between his teeth and administering a strong bite. "You know no one's gonna pay no mind to this muddy creek. Besides, Mr. Herndon says the railroad will be coming this way soon. He says one day it will stretch from one end of this country all the way to the other! There won't be a need for riverboats no more."

"Not if Abe would have won that politicing job! He told me he was going to vote to clear this river for even the big steamers to get through. He said I could've gotten a job on one of them."

"Ha! Jack, I don't know which one of you is a bigger dreamer, you or Abe Lincoln?"

As the boys sat on a rock ringing out the bottoms of their britches, Jack quietly stared at the gentle river that had become the object of his imagination. It was in the spring of this same year when he caught sight of his first steamer, the *Talisman*, chugging upstream toward Portland Landing.

Talk of navigating the narrow Sangamon River had begun spreading through Central Illinois years earlier. It was considered a potential trade route of great import; connecting the prairie of Central Illinois with the great Mississippi river a hundred miles to the west. With the western territories becoming increasingly more settled with each passing year, the need for a steady and dependable stream of supplies had become critical. Transporting them overland was an arduous and time-consuming endeavor, and required many trips to deliver the amount of supplies carried by a single steamer. Though narrow and crooked as a dog's hind leg, the Sangamon seemed a logical choice for promoting commerce. Efforts were even made to gain the support of President Andrew Jackson to dispatch the Corps of Engineers to clean out and widen the river's narrow passages.

And so it was, spurred on by the promise of a steady river trade, that James Rutledge and John Camron founded the small village of *New Salem* high on a bluff overlooking the Sangamon River. Soon, the state legislature granted them permission to construct a dam just below the village that was eventually used to operate a combination saw and gristmill. In a short time, with the mill drawing trade from miles around, the burgeoning little village welcomed the opening of the Hill-McNeil Store and Clary's Saloon. The added commerce quickly moved New Salem from a patch of uncut timber to a major frontier trading post. People moved to the village from all parts of the Eastern states; Jack Kelso from Massachusetts; the Bales family from Virginia; and the Herndons from Pennsylvania, to name a few. Some moved to the village with some purpose in mind, while others, by mere happenstance, found their way to New Salem during a journey westward.

Jack was fishing from the bank of the river that day when the sound of the Talisman blowing steam startled him to his feet. The sight of the ninety-five foot boat, its magnificent red paddlewheel leaving a path of frothing white water in its wake, became indelibly etched in his young mind. It was truly a breathtaking sight as it rounded the bend just upstream from the village. From that unforgettable moment forward, the idea of working as a deck hand on a steamer preoccupied his every dream and ambition. His eyes would sparkle at just the mention of an approaching steamer. And whenever the Talisman or another paddle wheeler would sound its call within earshot of the village, Jack would drop everything, regardless of what he was doing at the time, and make a quick dash to the riverbank to watch the approaching steamer round the bend and dock at a small clearing near the gristmill.

In the end, it seemed that President Jackson had more important issues to deal with than clearing the muddy Sangamon. The Corps of Engineers never showed up, and the river's many bends and passages were never cleared or widened. As a result, the larger steamers were never able to get beyond the major ports closest to the Mississippi and Ohio Rivers to the east and west. And while New Salem continued to see its share of small to medium sized steamers, including the Talisman, Jack's dream of working as a deck hand seemed to fade as interest in the river gradually became overshadowed by the slow but steady expansion of the railroads into the frontier territories. Jack knew the change was inevitable, in spite of his and Abe Lincoln's love for the river and its colorful and proud vessels. Such was the way of progress in 1830s America.

"Hey, Jack?"

"Huh?"

"If losing that penny is troubling you, I got something that will make you forget all about it." Finney pointed to the opposite side of the river where Becky Rutledge and Sally Armstrong busied themselves picking wild flowers. "I wonder if Becky Rutledge is picking those flowers for you, Jack?" Now, it was no secret to Finney that Jack harbored some mighty strong feelings for Becky Rutledge.

In an instant, Jack perked up like a prairie dog on his haunches. Straightaway, he shifted his gaze out across the river. Sure enough, Becky and Sally were busy filling their colorful baskets with little care for the goings-on around them. Jack followed Becky's every move, his heart beating faster with her every step. Then, as suddenly as a candle doused by a gust of wind, he slumped back into his glum demeanor with a heavy sigh. "Ah, she ain't got no interest in me."

"But you got a mighty big one in her, don't you?" Finney poked Jack in the ribs with a stick and laughed.

"What makes you say that?"

"Because, every time you get around her you lose all track of what you're doing."

The truth was, next to riverboating nothing grabbed Jack's attention more than Becky Rutledge. In his mind she was prettier than a wild prairie flower. The problem was, he could never bring himself around to tell her his true feelings. Each time he felt a compunction to do so, something always seemed to defeat his efforts; usually his own lack of self-confidence. It never seemed to quell his desire to be near her though in the off chance that by some divine power he might spew forth his feelings without inhibition. Unbelievably, at least to those who knew him, he even began sitting through Reverend Cartwright's Sunday sermons just to be close to her. Of course, this circumstance created its own set of problems. Becky always sat next to her parents in church—in the front pew! This meant that Jack found himself each Sunday morning, a time typically reserved for anything but church, sitting uncomfortably near the front and directly in the path of Reverend Cartwright's passionate delivery. It was surely no place for a boy to get much shut eye! The Reverend seldom remained behind the pulpit for any length of time. He was the type of circuit riding, frontier evangelist who endeavored to force God into the souls of unwilling or hesitant villagers through his fiery sermons. At even the hint of heavy eyes in one of his congregants, he would abruptly blurt out a loud "HALLELUJAH!" from just the right location to startle the drifter's attention back to the message at hand. Of course, if the guilty party's attention was captured not by sleep, but by a pretty young lady in her Sunday best—as you can reason Jack's was—then a private scolding by the Reverend following church, complete with a lecture on Biblical virtues, was in order. Jack was no stranger to the routine. He could well recite the relevant scriptures from memory.

"Hey, Jack! I have an idea."

"What?"

"You've been wanting Becky Rutledge to notice you, right?"

"I reckon it would be kind of nice," Jack conceded.

"Well, you see that beaver dam over yonder?" Finney pointed to a large pile of tangled sticks floating in the river just a stone's throw from where the girls were picking flowers. Beaver dams were a common sight up and down the muddy Sangamon. For a young boy, they offered an enticing, though ill-advised opportunity for adventure.

"Wait a minute!" snapped Jack. "You can just clear your mind of that thought. Last time we pulled that trick we got Mr. Graham's hickory stick across our bottoms!"

Mentor Graham was New Salem's only school teacher, and had a much deserved reputation for being long on discipline and short on patience; a reputation the boys needed little reminding of. Unfortunately though, young boys tend to lose sight of such realities when the opportunity to perpetrate a swell—though not advisable—deception on their school Master presents itself. They just seem to lose all proper judgment in such situations.

It had been one of those blistering hot summer days when the humidity is thick enough to cut with a knife, when Jack and Finney, while swimming just upstream from the gristmill, caught sight of Mentor Graham on the riverbank collecting insects. The plan came together quickly, almost as if the thought had occurred to both simultaneously. A few moments to prepare, then Jack signaled the plan into action with a nod of his head. Violently, they began to splash in the water as if they were both fighting to stay afloat. After causing enough commotion to catch their teacher's attention, the boys each took a deep breath, swam underwater, and quietly surfaced inside a nearby beaver dam.

The prank seemed quite hilarious until they looked through the sticks to see Mentor Graham, clothes and all, jumping into the river and swimming toward the spot where they had gone under. In a way, his concern for their safety, and, the boys reasoned, his desire to rescue them from their apparent predicament was a bit overwhelming. They had never before seen their dreaded teacher in such a caring light. As he quickly swam through the murky water to reach their location, the boys knew their dilemma was being compounded with each stroke. Both, without speaking, quickly abandoned any hope of getting away unscathed. Their only course seemed obvious. Like a puppy caught with the chewed remnants of a shoe still in his mouth, each exposed himself through the tangled branches and nervously awaited their fate.

Now, it is often true that young boys enter into such arrangements with very little thought or concern for the potential consequences. Foresight is simply not an exercise young boys employ with any degree of utility. Had they measured their idea with even the smallest bit of reason, chances are the next day in school they would not have felt such a burning in the area where their pantaloons met their chairs! Like so many times before, especially for Jack and Finney, it was lesson learned the hard way. In a frontier school, where the mischief and adventure that awaited the end of each school day could easily distract a young boy's focus away from the task in front of him, strict discipline was a necessary method. And no one doled it out more swiftly and with greater effect than Mentor Graham.

"Ah, come on," said Finney. "It'll give them a good scare."

"That's what I'm afraid of!"

"But don't you see? It's perfect!"

"How do you figure?"

"We'll make them think a river monster done got

hold of us."

"A river monster?"

"Sure! We'll swim inside that beaver dam over yonder, and just about the time they think we've been eaten alive, we'll swim on out and tell them we killed the critter." As Jack pondered the idea, a vision of Becky Rutledge kissing his cheek in admiration of his courage flashed before his eyes. Just the thought of it caused him to momentarily forget the penny now tucked safely away in Finney's pocket. *Perhaps the potential benefits did outweigh the risks,* he reasoned. After all, what was the worst that could happen; Becky getting angry and refusing to talk to him? Hmm... didn't seem like much of a risk given that she already paid so little attention to him that he felt practically invisible around her. Of course, if the scheme did by chance meet with success, Becky would no doubt shower him with her affections like a knight returning from battle. It definitely cast a different light on the proposition.

"What are we waiting for?" he asked, as he dove head first into the muddy water.

Quietly, the two swam to within ten feet of the beaver dam. The girls took no notice of the happenings, oblivious to the scheme about to be perpetrated on them.

"You ready?" whispered Finney.

"Ready? Why, I can already feel that river monster licking my toes!"

It was time to put their plan into action. As the boys began to splash violently and scream for help, the two girls, startled by the commotion, dropped their baskets and ran quickly to the river's edge.

"HELP!" screamed Finney. "It's a river monster!

He's got us both by the feet!"

"Oh my goodness!" gasped Becky. "Something's got Jack and Finney!" The girls grabbed each other in disbelief at the horrible spectacle playing out before their eyes.

"What'll we do!" screamed Sally, in a panic.

"I don't know!"

"Get back!" yelled Jack, in his most courageous voice. "It's too dangerous!"

At just the right moment the boys took a deep breath and disappeared together beneath the murky surface.

"Oh no!" cried Sally. "They've been pulled under!"

As the two girls watched in horror, Slicky Bill Green happened down the embankment toward the river. Slicky Bill had come to New Salem aboard the Talisman, and now spent most of his days either tending the counter at Abe Lincoln's store, or dropping a hook and line in search of ol' Mike, a catfish rumored to be the size of a grown man. Slicky Bill wasn't well known for ambition, but he was always good for a rib-tickling yarn or a game of checkers. It was the type of attitude New Salem just seemed to instill in its residents, especially the men among them. The sun never seemed to set on a hard day's labor without being interrupted a time or two for some friendly debate at Clary's Saloon, or perhaps a wrestling match or turkey shoot to allow the contestants to prove their manly prowess over a nickel wager. Regardless of the outcome, a handshake always preceded the payment. People had to depend on each other on the prairie. It was understood that a man never allowed night to fall with an apology owed.

"Slicky Bill! Slicky Bill!" cried the girls, as they ran toward him.

"Whoa there little ladies. Slow yourselves down so I can understand you."

"It's Salem Jack and Finnigan Reeves!" cried Sally, still in a panic. "Some critter grabbed them and pulled them under!" The girls grabbed Slicky Bill by both arms and pulled him toward the water's edge.

Slicky Bill quickly surveyed the situation. Being once a kid himself, there were two things he could recall holding a rather strong proficiency in. One was teasing girls—something that becomes second nature for nearly all young boys—and the other was swimming inside beaver dams. Now, there was just something in Slicky Bill's nature that made it difficult to give up a secret of such sacred origins, especially to girls. But as he scanned the embankment just upstream from the dam, it became obvious that the secret was about to be disclosed in an abrupt sort of manner anyway, and with no help from anyone.

"I wouldn't get too excited over it young'ns," said Slicky Bill, with a laugh. "The only critter them boys are going to see is that mama beaver over yonder." The girls turned to see a large beaver making its way toward the dam.

"Wonder what they're looking at?" asked Jack, as he peered through the sticks at Slicky Bill and the two girls.

"Beats me," answered Finney, oblivious to the unfolding event.

About that time the mama beaver swam into the dam, not expecting to find her home inhabited by two varmints the likes of Jack and Finney. From the bank of the river it sounded as though they truly had come face to face with a monster. Twigs and branches flew in all directions as the boys burst through the top of the dam with the angry beaver biting at the seats of their britches. In a moment, both were gasping for breath in the muddy river and kicking feverishly to escape the critter's wrath. With each spastic stroke, the girls' dander raised. Jack and Finney's devious plan was now fully exposed.

"Don't believe I've ever saw a boy swim that fast before!" said Slicky Bill, with a laugh.

"It wasn't funny from my point of view," said Finney, as he and Jack pulled themselves from the water. The quick swim had exhausted them both. Fortunately, the angry beaver had discontinued her aggressive chase and quietly returned to her den. A tear was evident in the seat of Finney's britches where the beaver's bite had found its mark.

"Finnigan Reeves!" snapped Sally with her hands on her hips and a rather dour look in her eye. "You nearly scared the curls right out of my hair!"

"Well then," interrupted Slicky Bill, not wanting to get caught in the middle of what was brewing. "I think I'll just wander downstream a stretch. They tell me ol' Mike's been jumping down around the sandbar of late." Out of sight from the girls, Slicky Bill offered the boys a wink and one of those grins that seemed to say he was glad it was them and not he in such a predicament. Finney just glared at Slicky Bill with a piercing look, unable to speak his true thoughts in the presence of the girls. Instead, he reasoned it best to start searching for a way out of the present mess his seemingly swell idea had gotten them into.

"Gee, Sally," began Finney, with all the charm his mud-stained smile could muster. "You suppose if I was to buy you a licorice stick up at Abe's, you might find it in your heart to forgive me?" Finney tilted his head toward Jack and winked in a cunning way.

"Well, I suppose I might consider it," answered Sally, with her soft hand outstretched. A slight smile signaled to Finney that his plan was working. Without hesitation, and in true gentlemanly form, Finney took Sally's hand ever so gently in his own, taking great precaution not to muddy her bright yellow dress. He was a master at charming the young ladies of the village, especially when it resulted in some personal reward. In this instance, not feeling Sally's wrath for attempting to scare them as they did was certainly a reward worth securing.

"After you, fair maiden." Finney's chivalrous invitation brought a sparkle to Sally's soft green eyes.

As the two departed, Jack stood quietly with his head pointed downward. As was usually the case whenever he got close to Becky Rutledge, he found himself speechless and unable to murmur even the slightest of trivialities. He nervously shifted from one foot to the other. It didn't much matter, he reasoned, that his courage had suddenly turned tail and skedaddled. After pulling such an ill-advised stunt, he figured Becky would never again speak to him anyway.

"Well, Jack?" asked Becky, in an impatient voice.

"Huh?"

With a sigh of frustration, Becky held out her hand. "Aren't you going to buy me a licorice stick? I happen to know Abe got a fresh supply on that wagon from Springfield this morning."

A sudden sense of excitement invaded his thoughts. He shook his head to clear any remaining water from his ears. Had he heard her correctly? Could it be? Here stood the girl of his dreams, her hand outstretched, offering him the opportunity to buy her a licorice stick up at Abe's store! Jack's heart began to beat rapidly as the reality of the situation set in. His mind raced, trying desperately to formulate a response to her sudden show of interest.

"Uh...uh...SURE!" he blurted, stuttering for his words. Then, as he was about to take her hand and set off to fulfill all his dreams wrapped up in this one instance, he remembered losing his only penny to Finney. Suddenly, his excitement gave way to panic! His disappointment quickly became mixed with a desire to avoid being humiliated at his usual lack of money. "Um...actually, I'd sure like to, but I've got to hurry on up to the saloon. Mr. Clary will be expecting me about this time."

"Suit yourself," responded Becky, flippantly. Without hesitation she swirled about and departed his presence. As she walked the path leading up the embankment and through the trees, Jack sat on a nearby rock with a look of total dejection etched across his face. He began skipping stones across the river's muddy surface. Out of the corner of his eye he could see Becky finally disappear from his sight. As she did, he sunk even deeper into his melancholy.

"You out there, ol' Mike?" he asked, with a particularly forceful throw. "I sure wish I knew your secret. You've got everyone in the village trying to catch you, and I can't get Becky Rutledge to show an interest in me for nothing'!" Jack considered Becky's demeanor toward him. "It wasn't me as much as it was that silly licorice stick she was wanting anyway."

Jack often came to the river's edge to sit on a rock and converse with ol' Mike. It was a place of solace, a place where he could escape the troubles of his heart. Unlike Finney, who had his mother and father, an older brother, and two older sisters to help ease his troubles, Jack had no one. His arrival in New Salem two years earlier had been by mere accident. It was during a move westward from Pennsylvania to the unsettled territories of Missouri when Jack and his family became lost in a blinding snowstorm on the prairie just north of New Salem. William Clary, who owned and operated the village's saloon, was on a return trip from Sandridge when he happened onto the young boy wandering aimlessly in the snow. Sadly, Jack had been the only one of his family fortunate enough to survive the freezing temperatures. Since that time, he had remained in New Salem, working at the saloon for room and board. What little money Jack had from time to time was usually earned doing odd jobs for people around the village. Having now no parents of his own, Jack in a sense became New Salem's adopted son. It seemed fitting when people around the village began referring to him as Salem Jack.

"It just doesn't seem right, ol' Mike," continued Jack, skipping another stone across the river. "I'm letting Finnigan Reeves get me up to my ears in mischief so I can get Becky Rutledge to notice of me, and now he's up buying Sally Armstrong a licorice stick while I sit here with one less penny in my pocket than when I started!" As if expecting a response, Jack quietly gazed out across the slow current. "Ah, it doesn't matter anyway!" As he got up to leave, he flung one last stone out across the river. "Huh? What was that?" The stone had hit something in the tall marsh grass on the opposite side of the river. Quickly, Jack picked up another stone and threw it at the same spot. Once again he heard a loud 'thump.'

"Hmm, don't sound like no log." Jack's curiosity lured him into the water. As he swam toward the source of the noise, this time taking precautions to avoid any floating driftwood, he began to make out what appeared to be the tail-end of a canoe sticking out of the weeds. In a few minutes his brisk stoke drew him near. Jack waded in the shallow water and pushed aside the tall marsh grass, startled to find not only a canoe, but an old man laying face down in it. "Excuse me, mister," he began, as he tapped the old man on the shoulder. "If you need a place to sleep, they've got some soft beds up at Rutledge's Tavern."

About that time, Jack looked down to see the unmistakable sight of dried blood on the old man's beaver skin coat. With a gasp, he jumped backwards in the water. "Ol' Mike," he began, after catching his breath. "I think we've got us a dead man here!" Slowly, he again approached the canoe and carefully began rummaging through the old man's belongings for some clue to his identity. "Maybe I should go get Abe or Slicky Bill?" he said to himself, as he opened a buckskin saddle bag. "Hey, what's this?" Jack pulled from the bag what appeared to be a piece of buckskin with a map inked on it. As he followed the faded arrows to the center of the map, he came to a large 'X', next to which were the unmistakable letters, 'G-O-L-D.'

"GOLD! Wow, this looks to be some sort of treasure map!" About that time a cold hand grabbed his wrist. "AGH!" Jack fell backwards with a look of terror on his face. With a gasp, the old man raised his head and stared Jack dead in the eye. It was the sort of look that pierced its way clean to the bone, and caused Jack to suddenly tremble in his boots!

"Beware of the Redlegs!" he forced from his lips. Before Jack could say anything, the old man took a final breath and slumped forward in his canoe. Jack watched the old man for a few moments for any sign of breathing. There was no further movement detected. He stood motionless in the shallow water attempting to think clearly. He couldn't recall ever seeing a man actually die right before his eyes. When it became obvious that the old man would speak no more, Jack remembered the piece of buckskin still clutched tightly in his hand. Slowly he raised it to his eyes.

"Ol' Mike?" he began, as an idea came presently to mind. "If this here map does lead to gold, I don't reckon the old man will have much use for it." A smile appeared on his freckled face as his fear suddenly subsided and his mind became occupied with visions of gold. "Just maybe my luck is about to change for once?"

As Jack waded in the waist deep water, he became lost in a fantasy of him and Becky Rutledge walking hand in hand into the Lincoln-Berry Store to purchase not only Abe's entire stock of licorice sticks, but also a hefty supply of colorful, round lollies. A cup of sweet sassafras would follow that, topped off by a handful of Abe's hardiest cashews, lightly salted and fresh out of a hot dutch oven! And that would be just the beginning. On Abe's next trip to Springfield, Jack would see to it that he returned with the prettiest dress this side of the Mississippi, and a hat to match! Becky would surely then shower him with her unbridled affections. He would make her feel like one of the Egyptian queens he had read about in one of Abe's history book. All the pretties a young lady dreams of having would be hers for the asking.

Suddenly, Jack was startled from his fantasy by the

sound of approaching voices. Upstream a short distance he could make out a canoe moving in his direction with two men aboard. Both were wearing long moccasins. With one glimpse of the peculiar foot coverings, the old man's warning suddenly had meaning. Jack recollected that 'Redleg' was the name used to describe a certain, ruthless kind of trapper who wore red moccasins that stretched clear to the knee. Jack had never come across many such men beyond the few who happened through the village from time to time on their way west, but he knew well their reputation for savagery. He recalled hearing the story of one Redleg who bit off a man's entire nose just for beating him in a game of poker! It was the sort of story that instilled a deep sense of fear of such men in the boys of the village. Whenever one passed through, usually to purchase supplies, the boys knew to keep their distance, and the men of the village knew not to provoke their wrath. It was well known and unquestionably believed that a Redleg would shoot or stab a man in the back for the slightest of reasons, and then quickly disappear down the river never to be seen again.

As the canoe approached, Jack ducked out of sight into the tall marsh grass. He couldn't be sure, but guessed that the Redlegs had something to do with the old man's demise. Perhaps it was the map they were after? With circumstances being as they were—a map presumably leading to gold, and its holder lying dead in a canoe with a lead ball in his back—it seemed a likely scenario. Suddenly, he felt as if he were in the wrong place at the wrong time. The more he considered the situation, the more he recognized the dangerous mix he now found himself in the middle of. He decided it best not to stick around to introduce himself.

About that time, before Jack could make a stealthy retreat, the Redlegs caught sight of the old man's canoe sticking out from the weeds. Quickly they paddled their own canoe toward it. As they approached, Jack quietly moved farther back into the marsh grass, still clutching the buckskin map. From such a short distance their fearsome appearance sent a chill up the back of his neck. He held his breath, trying his hardest not to be detected.

"He's deader than a possum, Coonrod," said the short, skinny man sitting in the front of the canoe.

"I already knowed that, you ignoramus!" yelled the heavier, bearded one to the rear. "Now make yourself useful and start looking for that map!"

As the Redlegs pulled alongside the old man's canoe and rummaged through his belongings, Jack quietly folded the map and stuck it inside his shirt. That being the object of their search, he certainly didn't want to be found holding it like a puppy with the remnants of the pie still evident on his nose. Something told him, especially given the old man's remedy, that these particular men would do a bit more than scold him for his errant behavior.

"It ain't here, Coonrod."

"T'ain't here neither." Coonrod pondered the situation. "Levi, I'm guessing someone up in that village is holding our map about now."

"I'm thinking you're right, Coonrod," answered Levi. "Look how them weeds have all been pushed away." Jack stood motionless in the tall marsh grass as the Redlegs looked in his direction. Even the slightest ripple of water would lead to his detection.

"Someone beat us to it," said Coonrod, shifting his

gaze away finally from the area where Jack stood. "Levi, tie the old man to his canoe and sink it. But first float it out to a deeper spot so no one happens upon it."

"What then?" asked Levi, as he began stringing rope around the old man's lifeless body.

"Then we're gonna pay a visit to that village and see if we can find our map."

Levi floated the old man's canoe far enough out into the river to send it a good twenty feet to the bottom, and then stuck a large knife through its thin layer of skin. He reasoned that long before the river ever lowered enough to expose their deed—something that occasionally happened with an extended drought—the catfish would already have had their way with the old man's remains. "Have a good journey, old man." In a few short moments the canoe disappeared from the water's murky surface.

"Whew!" said Jack to himself, as the two Redlegs paddled toward the opposite side of the river. He was sure if they had spotted him, they no doubt would have sent him to the bottom of the river with the old man. "What do I do now?"

As he came out of the weeds, he found nothing but a few bubbles where the old man and his canoe had floated only minutes earlier. "I've got to tell someone!" Jack considered just who he could tell. It would have to be someone he could trust not to tell the whole village. He knew that if word spread, the Redlegs would surely find out that it was he who had the map. Just the thought of waking from a dead sleep to see the faces of those two scoundrels standing over him made him shiver clear to the bone. He had to be mighty careful. He quickly ruled out the idea of giving the map to the Redlegs to avoid his own untimely demise. Given the criminal way in which they intended to acquire it, Jack didn't consider it a dishonest endeavor to keep it for himself. "I know, I'll tell Finney! He'll keep it a secret!" If there was anyone he could trust, he reasoned, it would be his best friend.

As he slowly began to swim back across the river, Jack's thoughts again turned to Becky Rutledge. Maybe his luck truly was about to change. Perhaps it was fate that brought the map into his possession? Or perhaps just a stroke of luck? Whatever the reason for both he and the map being in that place at that moment in time, Jack figured it to be a situation worth exploiting to his own benefit. "One thing is for sure, ol' Mike," he said, as he tucked the map in his shirt and began his swim back to the other side. "I'm figuring that gold is rightfully mine now, and no one is gonna steal it away from me. Not even them Redlegs!"

2

A PLAN IS HATCHED

By the time Jack climbed the steep bluff into the village his mind was running wild replaying the events that had transpired only moments earlier in the river below. The sight of the old man slumped forward in his canoe burned in his memory. He checked his hands for any remnant of the dried blood that covered the old man's coat. Even with no sign of the blood present, he rubbed his hands briskly against his pantaloons. His heart raced, as his thoughts bounced to and fro between the terror of nearly being spotted by the Redlegs, and the map now tucked safely inside his shirt. Quickly he scanned the village. Perhaps it was his imagination getting away from him a bit, but suddenly the village seemed unusually still. The sounds typically unnoticed by a young boy—birds chirping, bushes rustling, a squirrel scurrying up a tree—caused Jack's head to turn with his every step. Even Rutledge's Tavern, a place usually bustling with the comings and goings of frontiersmen in search of a hot bath and a soft bed, was quiet as he passed by. He kept an especially sharp eye for the Redlegs. He wanted to avoid them at all costs, hoping that in a short stretch of time they would give up their search and move on down the river.

"Hmm...I wonder where Finney is." He decided to try first the Lincoln-Berry Store, where he figured he'd find Finny and Sally Armstrong busying themselves with a tasty licorice stick purchased with Jack's hard-earned penny. The supply wagon from Springfield made its way to New Salem only every two weeks or so. For the village's youthful inhabitants, the idea was to have money in their pockets and at the ready when Abe restocked his candy jars, else they risked losing the opportunity to buy one of the tasty treats before they quickly disappeared, as was usually the case.

For Jack, it was the first time he had had money in his pocket in over a month. And while it certainly wasn't the first time he had lost his fortunes in an honorable way—a bet with his best friend—in this instance his defeat had caused him to lose out on a golden opportunity to be with the girl of his dreams. Just the thought of it caused an anger to build. He bit his lower lip to contain his agitation. At the same time, he reached inside his shirt to feel the piece of buckskin. "I'll show them!" he murmured. His newfound purpose caused him to quicken his pace through the village. He had to find Finney, and quick!

As he passed by Doc Allen's cabin, Jack's thoughts again turned to the old man in the canoe. He wondered about the old man's identity, and how it was that he came to have possession of the map. Perhaps it was he who had stolen it from the Redlegs? After all, he hadn't known the old man. Perhaps he was as ruthless and cunning as the Redlegs? As vicious as they appeared to be from his vantage point in the marsh grass, could it be that they were just trying to reclaim what was rightfully theirs? And if they were, was it proper for Jack to keep the map? Now it came to mind that the only method for Jack to truly solve the mystery of who owned the map would be to simply ask the Redlegs. Of course, this carried with it a certain amount of risk. What if they chose to lie? Worse yet, given their murderous way with the old man, what if they decided it best not to have any witnesses to the happenings in the river? Against all this, Jack weighted the benefits of possessing a cache of gold, no matter how small the quantity. As he walked in through the open door of the Lincoln-Berry store, he decided, at least for the present, to keep the map tucked safely away out of sight.

"Howdy Jack," said Abe, as he busied himself stocking the shelves of his one-room store with such items as cornmeal, beans, and coffee.

"Howdy Abe," answered Jack, looking around for any sign of Finney.

"Grab a chair and sit a spell. I'll be done in a short stretch." Abe stacked the last of the newly arrived supplies on his dusty shelves. Since his arrival in New Salem over a year earlier, he had become a close friend of Jack's, a big brother of sorts, and he always found the time to share a game of checkers or one of his rib-tickling yarns with him. No one could make Jack laugh quicker and with more force than Abe Lincoln. The two of them seemed to delight in each other's presence. Reverend Cartwright even referred to them once in a sermon as one, an older version of the other!

It was during a trip the previous year down the shallow Sangamon when Abe and his three crew-mates accidentally stranded their flatboat on the gristmill dam. Although they managed to free the boat by the next day and continue on to New Orleans to deliver their cargo, Abe's short stay instilled in him a hardy appreciation for the small village. Within days of making his delivery, he caught a steamer for St. Louis, from whence he walked the remaining hundred miles back to New Salem. With the idea of navigating the

Sangamon River gaining more widespread attention, Abe reasoned that New Salem would be an ideal locale from which to conduct trade and commerce. He also found the people there friendlier than any he had come across on the frontier, and the young ladies, especially one named Ann Rutledge, even prettier! She was Becky Rutledge's older sister, and not only was she resplendent in her beauty, but also well read in world history and the Classics.

Abe had met Ann while lounging one day on Jack Kelso's portico during his previous but short stay in the village. Jack Kelso was himself well read, especially in the works of William Shakespeare. No one seemed to know for certain where he came from. Like many in the village, he just strolled in one day in search of a hot meal, and then took a keen interest in staying. His small cabin was lined with the books he had purchased on his many trips to Springfield; books he often loaned to Ann Rutledge. She was returning one the day Abe laid his eyes upon her for the very first time. He immediately took an interest in her, and she in him, and he quickly set his mind to courting her upon his planned return. Some of the women about the village even whispered amongst themselves that she was the only reason Abe decided to return to the village. It was an allegation he never tried to refute with much passion.

"You haven't seen Finnigan Reeves, have you?" asked Jack, as he pulled a chair up to the counter.

"As a matter of fact, I have. He left here no more than five minutes ago with a smile on his face and Sally Armstrong on his arm."

"Smiling, was he?" Jack's irritation again surfaced.

"He sure was. Of course, he did say that you were the

one who was responsible for his good fortune." Abe struggled to hold back his smile. The corner of his mouth quivered as the need to bellow out a cackle began to swell. Knowing Jack as he did, he reasoned that he wasn't much too pleased at losing his only penny. For the moment, he purposed not to add salt to the wound by finding humor in Jack's misfortune. He knew Jack to be a sensitive sort; one who could perpetrate a practical joke with masterful perfection, but who, when the tables were turned, was seldom receptive to having the joke played on him.

"It wasn't me as much as it was that driftwood!" rebutted Jack. "Anyway, my sights are aiming a bit higher than a mere penny at the moment!"

"Well now," continued Abe, with a startled sort of look. "That doesn't sound like the Jack I know. Why, the Jack I'm acquainted with knows how to appreciate a penny!"

"Well, let's just say I've got a whole new outlook on life, Abe."

"A new outlook, eh? Sounds to me like a plan might be in the works. I don't reckon for a cup of sweet sassafras you'd be willing to tell me what it is?" Abe was a master at the art of conversation. He could almost always convince a young boy with a long face or a wily look in his eye to share his thoughts.

"I'd sure like to, Abe. But there are times when a man just has to keep things to himself. You know how it is."

"I reckon I do," answered Abe, pouring Jack a cup of the sweet sassafras and respecting his sudden need for secrecy.

Jack took a sip from the cup and then again placed

his hand on his shirt to feel the piece of buckskin underneath. He wondered if he should tell Abe about the old man in the canoe. Jack trusted no one more than Abe Lincoln. But this was a case of murder! Abe's first course of action would be to summon the constable to place the Redlegs under arrest until the Marshal could make his way from St. Louis. This would only increase the odds of the map's existence being discovered; perhaps even by the Redlegs own admission. Jack didn't know much about trials and such, but something told him that if the map was known to be in his possession, the Marshal would surely require him to hand it over. For the present, he decided to just keep it tucked safely inside the fold of his shirt, and his comments, even to Abe, a bit cryptic.

"Abe?" He hesitated for a moment, unsure whether to risk asking the question, but then blurted it out. "Have you ever heard tell of any gold being found in these parts?"

"Gold!" laughed Abe, as he placed his last bag of beans on the shelf. "What makes you wonder such a thing?"

"Oh, you know; just curious mostly." Jack tried hard to maintain a detached tone. He didn't want to draw Abe's attention to the reason for his inquiry. As he well knew, Abe was an inquisitive sort, and had a much deserved reputation for getting to the truth of a matter. His talent was God-given for the most part; the rest resulting from the countless hours he spent reading law books. Abe had grown quite fond of the written law, and had thoughts of joining the Springfield Bar one day. It was a lofty goal. To be admitted required that he pass an exam. And that meant a lengthy period of study. Abe was tireless when it came to reading and studying, and he never passed on the opportunity to practice his budding courtroom technique on his friends and neighbors.

"Hmm..." Abe leaned on the wooden counter across from Jack. "Well, I have heard tell of a strain of gold the size of a steamboat somewhere in these parts."

"A steamboat! That must be worth hundreds of dollars!"

"More like thousands."

"Wow!" Jack's excitement began to build. He envisioned a chunk of gold the size of the Talisman! Again he reached to feel the piece of buckskin underneath his shirt, making sure not to expose its presence to Abe. "So where is it?"

"No one knows for sure. Rumor has it that no one who ever set out for it ever returned." Abe glared into Jack's eyes. He was a skillful story teller, and even the most discerning adults routinely fell victim to his method.

Jack's blue eyes opened to the size of silver dollars.

"What do you think got them?"

"Hard to tell," answered Abe, scratching his chin.

"Some say the black curse fell upon them."

"The black curse?" Jack was hooked like a catfish on a trotline.

"Yup. You see, not so long ago the land all around us here belonged to the Kickapoo."

"You mean injuns?"

"In the flesh! Anyway, seems the Kickapoo held a special appreciation for gold. They used it to mold gifts and such for their spirit gods. When the white man decided to make these parts his own, well, let's just say the spirit gods were none too happy."

"The black curse?"

“You figured it! Those who claim to know the unknowable say it lays in wait for any poor soul who has a mind to stake claim to the gold.”

“Wow!” whispered Jack. Just the thought of it made him tremble, as he tried to envision the creature. There was little wonder why the gold was still out there waiting to be found! Jack couldn’t help but ponder how many in search of the precious rock had fallen prey to the curse’s murderous ways. Abe’s words had lulled him into a hypnotic state of sorts, so much so that he nearly jumped clean out of his boots when the sound of approaching footsteps startled him.

“Afternoon, Gents,” said Abe. The sight of the two Redlegs sent chills up and down Jack’s back! He quickly raised the cup to his face in an effort to conceal his skittish reaction. For Abe, seeing strangers pass through the village, especially the steady stream of frontiersmen journeying westward, was a common occurrence. “What might your pleasure be this fine day?”

“Dry goods, sir,” began Coonrod. “But first, you reckon we could catch a taste of a smooth Tennessee whiskey while we figure what we need?” The two Redlegs licked their lips, each with a look of anticipation covering his grisly face.

Now, in those days dispensing liquor required a special license. Although Abe’s business was groceries and other goods, he routinely violated the law by selling whiskey to the village’s thirsty. The practice was not looked upon favorably by Clary’s Saloon, which did have the proper license, but being the friends they were, no protest was ever registered. Besides, Abe more than made up for it. Each time an over-confident frontiersman passed through dead set on challenging any and all in the village to an arm wrestling match for a twenty-five cent wager, the Clary brothers would invariably call upon Abe to meet the challenge. Few could ever take him. Of course, the Clary boys, always looking to gain the advantage, would typically groom the frontiersman with a few shots of their finest whiskey before accepting the challenge and wagering their money on Abe's powerful right arm. For those in the Saloon who were also passing through the village and unable to resist the wager, Abe did his best to feign a lack of confidence and a fear of his challenger. With a cotton sleeve hiding the thick muscle of his upper arm, his convincing portrayal almost always caused a heavy wager to be placed on the doomed challenger. For their part in the deception, the Clary boys would take half the pot, with Abe gladly taking the other.

"Just happens I have a fresh stock," answered Abe. As he busied himself pouring two cups of the strong whiskey, Jack looked away, trying his best not to attract the Redlegs' attention.

"You sure are muddy for this being such a dry day," said Coonrod. He gazed at Jack with a piercing sort of look.

"Been swimming down in that river, have ye?"

"Who, me?" asked Jack, nervously.

"He wasn't expecting that wall to answer him!" said Levi, with a toothless grin.

Jack attempted to force a laugh. "Oh, the mud? Uh, well actually..." Like a cornered raccoon, Jack searched for a way out of his predicament. "What was that? Abe, did you hear that? Sounded like Finnigan Reeves hollering my name. I best go see what he wants!" Without looking back, Jack hurried out the door and set off on a dead run down the long path leading to Mentor Graham's one-room school house.

"Strange sort a boy," said Coonrod, as he took a drink from his cup of whiskey.

"Ah, Jack's a fine lad," said Abe. "He's just got a touch of the fever is all."

"The fever?" asked Coonrod.

"Gold fever. I haven't known a young boy yet who hasn't felt its pinch."

Coonrod emptied his cup with a single gulp. "A mighty fine whiskey it was, friend. What do we owe you?"

"Two bits between you," answered Abe.

Coonrod dropped a silver coin on the counter and turned to leave. As he did, Levi stood in place attempting to lick the remnants of whiskey from the bottom of his cup. "Good day to you, friend," he said, as he grabbed Levi by the ear and headed for the door.

"And a good one to you," answered Abe. He secured the cork back in the bottle of whiskey and returned it to its place on the shelf. "Hey, what about those dry goods you were wanting?" It was too late. Through the front window Abe could see Coonrod remove his coonskin hat and hit Levi over the head with it.

"You ignoramus!" he heard him say.

The oak tree under which Jack came to rest was a frequent visiting spot for the kids who attended Mentor Graham's school. It was hidden among the timber just enough so that it was out of view from the main path, yet close enough to the school that the kids could easily dash through the front door before Mr. Graham finished his customary eight bells, signaling the start of school. As Jack well knew, to be late for school meant getting your britches set ablaze by Mr. Graham's dreaded hickory stick. Few kids, especially the boys, ever made it to summer break without falling victim a time or two to his torturous methods!

The oak tree also served as a registry of past and present courtships. Its location made it a perfect spot for a boy to sneak a kiss from his favorite girl, away from the watchful eyes of Mr. Graham, Reverend Cartwright, or any of the village's other adults, all of whom would not hesitate to report the event to the appropriate parents. As Jack sat on a log and gazed up at the tens of hearts carved into the tree, he realized, perhaps for the first time, that none contained his name. Many contained Finney's, and an even greater number contained Becky Rutledge's. A jealousy began to swell, as if it were his name that rightfully belonged next to Becky's in the many roughly etched hearts.

"I'll show them!" Jack pulled the buckskin map from underneath his shirt and unfolded it. "I'll make Becky Rutledge the happiest girl this side of Springfield! And the richest!"

Now Jack was not what you would call overly superstitious, but as he traced with his finger the route from New Salem to the spot on the map marked by the letters 'G-O-L-D,' any thought of Becky Rutledge suddenly faded. His mind now became inundated with visions of a ghostly creature stalking unsuspecting souls by the light of the moon, its wolf-like fangs ready at any moment to sink deep into the pulsating heart of its victim. The hair on the back of his neck stood on end. He shook his head to clear his mind of such thoughts, but he quickly slipped back into the grasp of his imagination. He envisioned himself walking a dark timber path, his only light radiating from the full moon high overhead. He began to breathe faster and faster as he pictured a tall, dark form quietly stalking him. In his mind he attempted to run, only to find himself stuck tight in a quicksand-like terror. He could almost feel the creature's cold, deathly hand wrap around his neck, and its hot, rancid breath move across his face. Suddenly, as the sound of his beating heart reached its crescendo, the creature's illuminated eyes met his. And then...

"AGH!" Jack jumped a good ten feet from where he had been sitting on the log.

"What's got you all jumpy?" asked Finney, with a startled expression. "You look like you just saw a ghost!" Jack took a deep sigh of relief. "Finney, you ever sneak up on me again like that, the only ghost anyone is going to see is yours!"

"Ah, I was just having a laugh. Besides, I've been looking for you."

"Were you now? I seem to recall you having more important things to do than wasting your time with me; like buying Sally Armstrong a licorice stick with that penny you won in a crooked way!"

"Ah come on, Jack. Aren't you over that yet?"

"As a matter of fact, I am," answered Jack, with a confident smile. "Set your eyes on this!"

"What's that?"

"A map," answered Jack.

"A map?"

"Not any ordinary map. This here's a treasure map!"

"How do you figure?" Finney grabbed the piece of buckskin and scanned the faded ink markings.

"Look there by the X." Jack pointed to the spot on

the map. "It doesn't take a genius to figure what G-O-L-D spells."

"Gold? Hmm..." Suddenly, Finney became a bit more attentive. "Where did you get this?"

"You promise not to tell?"

"Jack, did you steal this map?"

"No, nothing like that!" answered Jack, with a nervous grin. "Well, sort of."

"What do you mean, sort of?" snapped Finney. "I've never known anyone who sort of stole something! You either did or you didn't!"

"Well, I didn't! Look, if you would just keep quiet for a minute, maybe I could tell you the story!"

"Jack, it's those stories of yours that always seem to get me into more trouble than I want to be in!" Finney's better senses warned him he'd best leave and forget he ever laid eyes on the piece of buckskin, but his curiosity, especially about the gold, refused to wane just yet. "Okay, I'm listening."

"Great!" blurted Jack, with a smile and a look of excitement. He sat back down on the log and began to tell Finney the story of the old man in the canoe and of his two close encounters with the Redlegs. His demeanor became even more animated when he gave an account of his conversation with Abe about the rumored gold. Since he purposed to convince Finney to journey with him to find and retrieve the precious rock, he figured it best not to make mention of the curse at the present time.

"So what are you going to do?" asked Finney.

"I have a plan. See, I'm thinking the two of us could find that gold. We could set out at first light. Two days by canoe and..."

"Now just hold on, Jack!" interrupted Finney. "Just suppose for a moment I did want to go with you, which I haven't made known yet, what makes you think my pa will let me go?"

"It won't matter! See, I'm figuring if you were to just leave a note saying you went trapping for a few days, your pa will only be angry until he sees you coming through the door with an arm full of gold."

Finney laughed. "It's a sure thing you've never been near him when he's hollering mad!"

"Ah, come on, Finney. Think about it. Isn't there something your pa has been wishing for? Something a hefty big strain of gold could buy for him, and still have plenty leftover for yourself?"

Finney pondered the question. "Well, I reckon he has had his eye on a new plow for nearly as long as I can remember. The old one won't hardly break sod no more, no matter how much he sharpens it."

"Well then, there you go!"

Finney sat quietly on the log for a moment and considered the proposition. "Jack? Something tells me this is not a good idea. And it sounds like those Redlegs will skin us like jackrabbits if they catch us."

"In or out?"

Finney hesitated. "In, I reckon."

"I knew I could count on you, partner!" said Jack, as he spit in the palm of his hand and offered it in the customary manner.

"Jack, I'll never figure out how I get myself into these predicaments!" said Finney, as he followed suit and gathered up a spit.

After consummating their plan with a handshake, the boys set out to plan the more practical aspects of locating, mining, and bringing back in a canoe a strain of gold the size of a steamboat! With their sights set only on the expected treasure, little thought was given to the logistical constraints of such an endeavor. They figured that if the load was too heavy they'd simply leave some behind and return for it later. Between them they had the necessary tools, and Jack had access to a fine canoe that Mr. Clary kept tied to a tree just downstream from the gristmill. Of course, it would be necessary to take the canoe without Mr. Clary's blessing. Like Finney's father, to inform Mr. Clary of their intentions would no doubt bring a quick end to their planned expedition.

"Meet me by the canoe at first light," said Jack. "And bring some of your mama's sugar biscuits. We'll get hungry along the way."

"Jack, something tells me if I return without that gold you claim to know is there, my pa is going to make it hard for me to sit for quite a spell!" Finney didn't much want to consider such a prospect.

"Trust me, Finney. When your pa sets an eye on that gold, he may never give you another whipping forever!" Jack reasoned by the look on Finney's face that Finney wasn't as optimistic as he was about their chances for success. "Oh and by the way, do you still have that lucky frog's leg you won from Jimmy Clay?" He decided not to tell Finney about the black curse until they were a good piece downstream. He had no way of knowing whether a proven good luck charm would work against such a beast, but decided it wouldn't hurt to have it along.

"Got it right here in my pocket," answered Finney. "Why are you asking?"

"Oh, no reason. Just figured it wouldn't hurt to bring it with you."

"I planned on it," said Finney. "But if you're so sure about that map, I'm wondering why you would want my lucky frog's leg?"

"Like I was saying," answered Jack, trying not to alarm Finney to his concern. "No reason."

After swearing to secrecy, and to bring along a hardy supply of his mother's sugar biscuits, Finney disappeared into the timber. Jack placed the buckskin map back inside his shirt and quickly walked toward Clary's Saloon, keeping a sharp eye for the Redlegs each step of the way. He wasn't sure if they were on to him or not, especially after his nervous performance at Abe's store. For now, he wanted to avoid them at all costs.

Clary's Saloon was located high on a bluff just above the gristmill, and was a favorite gathering spot for the more boisterous, sporting crowd who routinely participated in such games as arm wrestling and cockfighting. For Jack, Clary's Saloon was home. The arrangement since his arrival in New Salem was a simple one; Mr. Clary provided Jack three meals a day and a warm bed in return for his promise to keep the wood box full and the floor clean. It was a difficult job at times, but one that Jack enjoyed for the most part. Mr. Clary and his brothers had become like family to Jack. And those who frequented the saloon treated Jack like one of their own. At one time or another they taught him how to carve small animals from twigs, to throw a tomahawk with deadly precision, and even how to sucker an unsuspecting gambler with a deck of cards and a little sleight of hand. Of course, his close association with the boys at Clary's Saloon did cause concern among the women of the village, most of whom considered it inappropriate for a young boy to be exposed to such sinful vices as poker and drunkenness. Even Reverend Cartwright occasionally seen fit to administer to Jack a double portion of bread and wine during Sunday Communion!

By the time the moon replaced the sun in the sky, Jack had gathered and packed all the necessary items for the morning's journey. As he lay on his bed in the small room to the rear of the saloon, he once again focused his attention on the map, the large 'X' barely visible in the dim candlelight. Many thoughts came to mind as he pondered the events of the day; the old man in the canoe; the Redlegs; the map he now held in his hands; the black curse; and of course, Becky Rutledge. But one other thing that had quietly crept into Jack's thoughts since meeting with Finney under the oak tree, and which up to this point had been quietly pushed to that darkened region of the mind reserved for uncomfortable memories, was Mrs. Reeves' sugar biscuits. It was true that nothing in the village was more delectable to the taste, but for Jack they were special for another reason. Mrs. Reeves' sugar biscuits reminded him of those his own mother made most every Sunday morning. A smile reached across his face at the thought of how even Sunday school seemed bearable with a belly full of the tasty gems. As his mind wandered, allowing him to return to a happier time, the buckskin map slipped from his fingers and onto the floor. Soon his eyes grew heavy, as the candle grew dark. The idea of finding gold had faded suddenly into the realm of lesser important thoughts.

3

THE JOURNEY BEGINS

It seemed a near perfect day for journeying downstream as Jack loaded a pick, a shovel, and a small bag containing such items as rope, matches, and beef jerky onto the canoe. It had taken a good bit of stealth to get the items out of the saloon undetected. With Mr. Clary being an early riser, Jack had to first drop the items through the opened window next to his bed before slipping quietly through the front door to retrieve them and journey on to the river's edge. Once there, he quickly spotted the canoe tied to a tree in its usual location. His excitement seemed to compound by the minute in anticipation of their departure. In the fresh morning air, with the sun barely creeping above the horizon, even the supposed black curse seemed less an obstacle as it had the day before. Besides, with Finney's lucky frog's leg close at hand, Jack felt reassured that the creature's wrath could be thwarted. With a vision of gold lingering in his thoughts, the curse seemed, at least for the time being, a risk worth taking.

"It's about time you get here!" snapped Jack, as Finney walked swiftly down the bluff toward the canoe. "We could've been all the way to Petersburg by now!" Jack knew the quicker they headed downstream the likelier they were to avoid contact with anyone from the village. Most would recognize Mr. Clary's canoe, not a small number of whom would surely question the boys' actions at such an odd hour and risk bringing a quick end to their journey.

"Ah, quit your complaining!" snapped Finney. "It isn't easy sneaking when your pa never seems to sleep!"

"Did you leave the note?"

"Yup. Laid it by his smoking pipe when he went out to gather eggs. He nearly had me when I tripped over that bucket!"

"Reckon he's on to you?"

"Naw. I heard him mumble a word or two about the old tomcat. We better hurry though. I expect he'll be firing up that pipe anytime now." Finney quickly, but carefully climbed into the canoe and took a seat to the rear.

"Did you bring everything?" asked Jack.

"Right here." Finney opened his bag to reveal an assortment of candles, string, a large knife, and at least half a dozen plump sugar biscuits. "And keep your hands off the sugar biscuits till I say you can have them!" Finney abruptly closed the bag before Jack could peer in to catch a glimpse of the scrumptious sweets. "I don't want them all ate before we even lose sight of the gristmill." On the prairie nothing was more delectable to the taste, especially the taste of a young boy with a seemingly bottomless stomach, than fresh sugar biscuits! They were simply impossible to resist once you caught a whiff of their aroma wafting through the air.

"I wasn't hungry anyway," answered Jack, trying to act indifferent to the treats as he busied himself with the canoe. At the same time his mouth watered at just the thought of biting into one of the tasty gems. In his haste to race to the river, taking great precautions to avoid Mr. Clary along the way, he forgot to eat the piece of leftover apple pie he had set aside the night before. Although he did manage to remember the small bag of jerky, at such an early hour the dried beef did little to satisfy his craving. For now, he reasoned it best not to quibble over the sugar biscuits. With Finney's father probably already reading the note, a hasty departure took priority over his growling belly.

It was a slow current as the boys set out from the riverbank. An early morning mist still hovered just above the water's surface. Only a single blue crane made its way lazily across the sky above. He took no notice of the boys' canoe as they began their trek downstream. For Jack, the excitement seemed to build with each stroke of his oar. He felt like a great explorer in search of an exciting new world. He reached to his chest to feel the piece of buckskin tucked safely underneath his shirt. As Finney nervously looked back through the timber, expecting to see his father break through at any moment, Jack recalled the story of Lewis and Clark that Mr. Graham had made them read aloud in school. At that moment he wished he had taken greater care to listen as it was being read. He considered that perhaps a story would be written about him and Finney's brave and magical journey one day! Just the thought of it caused him to sit upright in the canoe and paddle with a prideful stroke. He was sure that if Becky Rutledge could see him at that moment she would worship his bravery with her affections. His mind wandered, as he envisioned a large heart carved into the oak tree at its highest reachable spot, the poetic words Becky loves Jack etched for all eternity inside its unbroken border.

"Tell me something, Jack?" Finney's inquiry prompted no reaction. Jack continued stroking his oar through the thick current, deep in his thoughts. "Jack? Yoo-hoo, Jack?"

"Huh, you say something?"

"I surely did. Do you have bugs in your ears, or what?"

"Naw, I was just thinking." A smile lingered as Jack returned to the present.

"Well in that case, why don't you do some thinking about just where it is we're heading."

"Already did," said Jack, as he pulled the piece of buckskin from underneath his shirt. "According to the map, first we go as far as where the Salt Creek spills into the Sangamon. Then we paddle west till we come to a fork in the river."

"A fork? How do we know which way to go from there?"

"Like I was saying, I have it all figured. The map says the fork that wanders off to the north is Possum Creek. We just follow it till we come to a big rock in the water."

"What then?"

"I reckon that's where we tie down," answered Jack. "According to the map, that's where we'll find the gold."

"Jack, I surely do hope you ain't misfiguring your directions none." Finney didn't appear so confident of the outcome. Like most of Jack's schemes, Finney recognized the risks present in this one; the biggest being the usual probability that Jack's brilliant idea would in the end prove to be less than brilliant! The trouble was, it was usually Finney who paid the heaviest toll for Jack's mischievous plans. You see, Jack never had to worry much about discipline, at least not the kind typically doled out by parents; the kind that can leave a boy ravaged by a sense of shame and guilt. Jack's discipline was more of a business arrangement. The more he got into trouble, the more Mr. Clary made him sweep the floors, wash the dishes, and carry in the fire wood. Finney on the other hand had his father to contend with. And while it was no laughing matter to end up on the frayed end of his swatting stick, to make matters worse, Finney's father had a way of transforming his usual teeth-clenching anger at getting swatted in the backside, into a strange sense of self-blame. He hated the way his father always seemed to achieve that particular end. And he hated even more how Jack always seemed to escape the same emotional trauma for his mischievous deeds.

By the time the boys lost sight of the gristmill behind them, the sugar biscuits had long since disappeared into their growling bellies. The smell was just too tempting for both of them. As hard as Finney tried to fight the desire to bite into one of the sweet biscuits, in the end he was the first to fall to his weakness. How could he argue when Jack quickly followed his example and reached in the bag to partake of the delicacy? Within minutes they were just a memory.

"Well Jack, so much for rationing our food. We ate every one of them."

Jack held his belly, as the biscuits now caused it to swell. "I don't reckon I'll need anything more to eat till sometime tomorrow!"

"HA!" laughed Finney. "Jack I know how you eat! You're belly will be growling for more by noontime."

"I can't help it I get hungry," responded Jack. "I ain't lucky like you."

"What do you mean by that?"

"I mean, I don't get to wake up every day and taste the kind of cooking your mama's known for."

"Believe me Jack, having a mama who cooks like

mine isn't such a good thing sometimes."

"Now how could that be?" asked Jack. He couldn't imagine a downside to such a circumstance.

"Because, since none of her cooking is bad, you're just always expected to eat it like there's none better!"

"So what's wrong with that?"

"I'll tell you what's wrong with that, she don't seem to know the difference between the good kind of food and the bad kind sometimes."

"You mean collard greens?" Jack's face contorted.

"I mean collard greens, turnips, and even beets! And because she's such a good cook, well, it just sort of takes away your reason for not wanting to eat whatever she puts on your plate."

"I see your point," answered Jack, still a bit repulsed at the thought of being forced to eat such uninviting dishes.

In the slow current, it took nearly an hour to reach Petersburg three miles to the north. Those unfamiliar with the small outpost were at risk of passing by without even noticing it nestled quietly in the dense trees lining the embankment. The village included only a few cabins and a small blacksmith shop. There was no post office. Mail destined for the area was delivered by the postmaster in Springfield once a week to the post office at New Salem for the village's few inhabitants to pick up.

Both of the boys had been to Petersburg several times in the past, but neither could boast having journeyed much farther. Beyond the small outpost's perimeter was mostly unsettled territory all the way north to Peoria on the Illinois River, and west to Hannibal and Quincy on the great Mississippi. It was an area rumored to be still inhabited by small bands of the prairie Indians who once flourished in the region. Like most young boys with an insatiable need to explore the unknown, Jack was passionately intrigued by the accounts he had heard of the endless caverns, white water rapids, and sheer rocky cliffs that dominated the northern territory's landscape. Many times while sitting in deep contemplation by the lazy Sangamon he had felt a strong yearning to set out on a grand adventure. His fantasy was to set a course westward and move about like the blowing wind, free and unbounded, never staying in one place for too long a time. Unfortunately his desire for adventure always seemed hindered by one circumstance or another, usually Mr. Clary's demanding workload or Finney's lack of interest in risking the skin on his backside for one of Jack's ill-conceived ideas.

As they paddled their canoe slowly past the few cabins located near the bank of the river and just inside the trees, a silence befell them. Suddenly, they were in a strange place. They now noticed things around them normally taken for granted in a familiar setting; the wind passing through the trees; the sounds of the birds and insects; even the slightest rustling of the grass and bushes. Little was said as the eery silence engulfed them. Another blue crane, or perhaps the same one, lumbered its way across the sky. Even the water was strangely quiet as both of the boys lifted their oars and allowed the canoe to drift along in the slow current. Now one thing can be said of the muddy Sangamon; one cannot paddle for a great distance without the river bending in some different and odd direction. That perhaps was the reason Jack and Finney had no awareness of the canoe that had quietly been shadowing them since their departure, always one bend behind and out of sight.

"Finney?" asked Jack, after a long silence.

"Huh?"

"Have you ever kissed a girl?"

"Are you kidding? Of course I have!" Finney attempted to answer the inquiry with an air of confidence.

"Now I don't mean your sister or your mother." Jack qualified his question. "I'm talking about a real girl. And on the lips!"

"I knew that's what you meant."

"Well, what's it like?"

"You mean you haven't?" asked Finney, with a slight laugh.

Now young boys being as they are, Jack did not want the whole village, or even his best friend for that matter, knowing that he had never come even close to kissing a girl. It just wasn't the sort of information he wanted widely circulated!

"Of course I have!"

"Then why are you asking what it's like for?"

Jack hesitated, trying to figure a way out of his predicament. "I was just testing you," he said, finally. "See, I figure if you were telling the truth, then you must know what it's like." It wasn't the best explanation, but given Finney's need to prove beyond all doubt his proficiency at kissing girls, it seemed to work just fine in this instance.

"Well then, I'll prove to you I know. Kissing a girl, and I mean a real girl, is like biting into a lemon…kind of wet and sour." Jack's face contorted at the thought of it. "Now," continued Finney. "Is that proof enough for you?"

"I suppose," answered Jack. "Besides, I already knew you had. I saw your name carved into all those hearts on the oak tree."

"Yeah, I reckon there is a mighty big bunch of them," said Finney, with a lofty smile. "Probably even more than I know about!" He began to paddle with a certainty to his stroke. "How many do you have, Jack?"

"How many what?" he asked, in a sudden panic.

"You know…hearts! How many have your name in them?"

"Oh, I don't know," answered Jack, trying to act ignorant of the truth. "I done lost count a long time ago!"

As the boys continued on, stroking their oars in the slow current, Jack wondered if kissing Becky Rutledge could possibly be like biting into a sour lemon. In his mind, it had to be more like one of Mrs. Reeves' sugar biscuits; full of sweetness, and with a soft sort of texture about it. The truth was he didn't much care. He considered that a lemon is only sour for the first bite. He figured that if he could just get past the first kiss, the rest would be easy. The more he pondered the prospect, the quicker he paddled. At the same time his mission to retrieve the gold became clearer in purpose. He just had to have Becky Rutledge all for his own! He knew that without the gold his chances of ever achieving that goal would be lost.

"Jack," began Finney, after a few moments of silence. "Why don't you bait up a hook so we don't have to eat jerky for supper."

"What did you bring for bait?" asked Jack, as he pulled the hook and line from Finney's bag. Red worms and chicken gizzards were known to work best in the muddy Sangamon.

"What do you mean, what did I bring? I thought you

were bringing the bait?"

"Now why would I be bringing the bait when you're the one bringing the hook to put it on?"

"I swear, Jack. How are we ever going to find a strain of gold when we can't even decide who's bringing the chicken gizzards to fish with?" Finney rolled his eyes and let out a heavy sigh.

True to Finney's prophecy, Jack felt a hunger overtaking his belly. Any remnant of the sugar biscuits was now unnoticeable. Jack sat for a moment, then pulled his oar from the water and began removing his shirt.

"Jack, what are you doing?"

"If we can't catch some mud bellies on a hook," answered Jack. "Then I reckon we'll just have to hog them!"

"Hog them! Jack, I've never hogged a catfish, and I'm not planning on starting now. I've known too many men who've lost their fingers to a hungry snapping turtle! No siree, you're not going to get me to reach my hands into that muddy water snooping around for something I could have caught on a hook if you would've brought the bait!"

"Well then, I reckon I'll just have to do it myself," said Jack, as he unbuttoned his britches. "Paddle over to that tree in the water."

Hogging catfish is not an endeavor for the weak at heart. It is an uncomplicated task. You simply reach your hands into submerged logs and feel for sleeping catfish. Unfortunately, finding the critters is the easy part. The difficulty is in trying to get them from underneath the water and into your boat. There are two inherent obstacles to doing this. First, the only catfish that will lay still long enough to have a rope threaded through its mouth and out its gill is one that is too old and too big to much care...that is, until you give the rope a good tug. Those who have experienced the feeling of hanging onto a forty-pound catfish, irritated at having been awakened from a much needed state of dormancy, will tell you that it is comparable to riding a bucking bronco! To make matters worse, as many a fine hogger have painfully discovered, more than just catfish prefer to take up residence in the hollowed-out logs that cover the river's bottom. Although there were many ways one could lose a finger in a pioneer village such as New Salem, the vice-like jaws of a hungry snapping turtle certainly claimed its share of victims.

"Jack, are you sure you know what you're doing?" asked Finney, as Jack jumped from the canoe into the waste-deep water.

"Yup. I've watched Jack Kelso and Slicky Bill do it a hundred times. It's easy."

As Finney watched quietly from the canoe, Jack slowly lowered his hands into the muddy water. In a slow and methodical manner he moved his hands across the submerged timber looking for an opening in one of the larger logs. It was true that he had watched others hog catfish a time or two, but he had never attempted it himself. Out of fear of coming face to face with a hungry snapper, he curled his fingers inward so they didn't protrude so far outward.

"You feel anything yet?"

"Nope. Just a bunch of dead limbs." Beads of nervous sweat began to form on Jack's forehead. He never would have attempted such a hunt back in the village. But the idea of spending the next few days with no food, especially with the signs of hunger already making their way to the surface, sparked in him a newfound, albeit foolish, sense of courage.

"Well, while you busy yourself catching dead limbs, I'm going to catch some shut-eye." Finney lay back in the canoe and rested his head on his hands. Rising at such an early hour was beginning to exact its toll, as he let out a loud yawn. Within minutes he was drifting off under the mid-day sun. As he did, Jack quietly continued his search for an unsuspecting mud belly. Suddenly, as he reached into one particular hollowed-out limb just below the water's surface, he felt something move against the back of his hand.

"Finney! I think I've got one!"

"Huh...what?"

"I said, I think I've got one!"

Finney perked up in the canoe, now taking the situation a bit more serious. "You need the rope?"

"I don't know," answered Jack. "It feels kind of strange. Sort of like...like...OH NO!" Jack pulled his hand out of the water to find a large blacksnake coiling itself around his arm. "AGH!" With one swift motion of his arm, Jack flung the snake through the air and directly onto Finney's lap.

"AGH!" screamed Finney, as he jumped from the canoe and into the muddy water! Frantically he splashed his arms and legs in an effort to escape the serpent's company. No one hated snakes more than Finney. The feel of their slimy bodies sent chills up his back. At a safe distance from the canoe he coughed to free his mouth of the muddy river water. "Why did you do that?" he asked, his heart still beating rapidly.

"It wasn't on purpose," responded Jack, a slight grin now apparent. "Besides, it's just an old blacksnake. There's no reason to get all scared about it." Jack rather enjoyed watching Finney startled from his slumber.

"You weren't scared?" asked Finney.

"Ha! Of an old blacksnake?" Jack laughed at the suggestion.

"Well, if you weren't scared, then why did you throw it?"

"I thought I had a water moccasin on my arm!"

"You did, did you?" Finny asked, in a skeptical tone of voice. He wasn't buying Jack's dubious explanation.

"I surely did!"

"Well I don't remember ever seeing a water moccasin that looked so much like a blacksnake!" At that moment, having finally calmed a bit, Finney had an idea. "I reckon we best get it out of the canoe so we can be on our way."

"Yeah, I reckon so," answered Jack.

Finney waded up to the canoe and cautiously reached in to grab one of the oars. Now, it is true that young boys have less of a fear of snakes, especially harmless blacksnakes, than most people, but even young boys seem to shy away from those that are big enough to swallow a small animal, as this one was. Slowly, Finney placed the handle of the oar on top of the blacksnake and watched as it wrapped itself around the long, skinny piece of wood.

"It sure is a big one, Jack!" Finney played the drama like a Shakespearean actor.

"What's it doing?" Jack made no effort to move closer to the canoe. His close encounter with the snake now convinced him to keep some distance between them.

"Your eyes won't believe it!" continued Finney, trying to hide his devious grin. "It's swallowing the oar whole! Quick, come here and take a look!"

Jack slowly waded back to the canoe with a look of hesitation on his face. He had no great desire to see the big reptile again. Finny kept one eye on him as he approached. Then, at just the right moment, as Jack came to within throwing distance, Finney flipped up the oar and tossed the blacksnake directly at him with great precision.

"AGH!" Jack frightfully backpedaled through the water attempting to escape the slimy creature. Only his arms and hands were visible above water as he tripped over a submerged log and fell backwards. As Finney laughed loudly, the terrified snake gathered its senses and quickly wiggled its way out of sight. "What did you do that for?" yelled Jack, as he came up out of the water.

"It wasn't on purpose," answered Finney, sarcastically. "Besides, it's just an ol' blacksnake. No reason to get all scared about it."

"Real funny!" snapped Jack, as he angrily climbed back into the canoe. "If you're not too busy playing practical jokes that ain't the least bit funny, I'd suggest you get back in this canoe so we can get on downstream!"

"Okay, okay," Finney climbed back into the canoe with the smile still present on his face. "I take it you've given up on the idea of hogging catfish?"

Jack hastily put his oar back in the water and began paddling. "I haven't given up on anything. I just figure it's best if we don't stay in one place too long."

"What about dinner?" asked Finney.

"If you want catfish, or any other kind of fish, then you need to find something to bait a hook with!"

Finney looked around in the canoe. "Well, I've never fished with jerky before," he said, as he began to bait a hook.

"But I suppose catfish will eat just about anything."

Jack tried to maintain his anger toward Finney. Although in hindsight the spectacle was rather comical, he was determined for the moment not to let on that the gag had gotten the best of him. To do so would be to admit defeat, an unthinkable act for a boy with a competitive nature such as Jack's was. Rather, he schemed for the moment to lay patiently in wait for Finney to drop his guard just enough to make himself vulnerable to Jack's quick and creative knack for returning a practical joke. With their adventure still young, there would be plenty of time for such amusement.

By the time they reached the small settlement at Sand Ridge, Jack's self-imposed silence had long since met its end. Their thoughts and conversation now centered on one thing...the gold! As they fantasized about the many and splendid ways they could spend their anticipated fortunes, even Finney's eyes began to sparkle a bit with excitement. The thought of having an unlimited amount of money in their pockets was a bit overwhelming. Both felt as though they had been presented a once in a lifetime opportunity. It was truly the type of circumstance they had only read about in books, or heard about in the tall tales of passing travelers and frontiersmen.

One additional circumstance had also crept into Jack's thoughts as they drew nearer their destination. Having Finney's lucky frog's leg close at hand seemed to ease his mind somewhat about the unknown that lay ahead, but Jack knew that out there somewhere the black curse lay patiently in wait for their approach. Again he tried to imagine the creature's hideous appearance. As his mind wandered, the sound of Finney's voice faded into the darkness of his thoughts. His paranoia caused him to suspiciously scan the timber lining both sides of the river. Being as close as they still were to Petersburg, he reasoned they were in safe territory for the time being. But by nightfall, even in the slow current, they would find themselves in an area to which neither had journeyed before. Although he hoped to avoid any situation that would demand their reliance on a good luck charm's unproven powers, one thought of Becky Rutledge was enough for Jack to convince himself that the black curse was a risk worth taking

4

ALONE IN THE WILDERNESS

"How many miles you reckon we've gone?" asked Finney, as he pulled his oar from the water and wiped the sweat from his brow. The late afternoon sun was beginning to take its toll on the boys as they lumbered along in the slow moving current. Not even a slight breeze could be detected.

"I'd guess at least thirty," answered Jack. "It shouldn't be much further to the Salt Creek." By now the terrain had changed rather dramatically. High rocky cliffs now cast their eerie shadows across the water. Even the river itself had changed in appearance, suddenly narrowing with small fingers branching off in all directions. They had seen no sign of life since passing by Sand Ridge hours earlier. They surmised that the river had by now parted ways with the major routes of travel north to Peoria and Ft. Dearborn. They well knew that only seasoned frontiersmen departed those routes for fear of the dangers the wilderness held.

"I don't suppose it really matters much," said Finney, exhausted from the day's journey. "My pa has probably decided by now to give me a whipping like I never had before!"

"Ah, he'll change his mind when he sees you coming home with a load of gold in your arms," said Jack, trying to soften a bit Finney's perception of his expected consequences.

"Jack, what makes you so sure we're going to find that gold? I mean, that "X" on that piece of buckskin covers a mighty big area."

"As a matter a fact," began Jack. "I've been thinking about that very thing. The way I see it, if that old man already dug for it, he surely left a hole behind."

"What makes you think he already dug for it?"

"Because," answered Jack. "I don't recollect seeing any digging tools in that canoe of his."

"Maybe he was going to buy some? He could've purchased some tools in the village."

"How do you figure he would've bought them?" asked Jack. "I'm thinking if that old man would've had money in his pocket to buy digging tools, then those Redlegs surely would've taken it! I didn't see either of them doing any such thing. And I didn't see any furs in the canoe for the old man to trade with."

It was true that on the frontier, furs were as good as currency at times. Trappers and hunters routinely used them to barter for the necessary supplies to sustain them through their efforts. They were used for clothing, for blankets, to cover the cold wooden floors of cabins, and to line the insides of boots for warmth and waterproofing. With currency difficult to come by on the prairie, local economies appreciated the worth of skins and furs, and placed as much trade value on them at times as chickens and freshly stilled whiskey!

"Well, if he did already dig for it, why didn't he just take it with him the first time?" Finney continued his inquiry.

"I've been asking myself that question. I'm figuring

there was too much to take. Or maybe he already took one load and was returning for another?"

"Or maybe," blurted Finney sarcastically. "He just found that map where someone who knew it didn't mean anything threw it!"

"Maybe he did," conceded Jack. "But one thing's for sure. We're never gonna know if that gold is really there unless we look for it ourselves."

"Jack," began Finney, as he lowered his oar back into the water. "Something tells me the only thing we're gonna find there is a whole lot of trouble!"

"Ah, quit your complaining," answered Jack, as he too returned his oar to the water and continued on in the hot sun. "'Besides, it's not like I never had a good idea before."

"Ha!" laughed Finney. "Now that is a stretch if ever I heard one, Jack!"

"It wasn't meant to be a stretch!" Jack wasn't amused at Finney's sarcasm. "How about the time I built that sled to slide down Johnson Hill on?"

"Now that truly was a fine idea," laughed Finney. "In fact, it was such a fine idea you might recall Billy Perkins breaking both his arms on those rocks you forgot was under the snow!" From his seat in the rear of the canoe, Finney shook his head and continued his goading laughter.

"Oh yeah," said Jack, a bit embarrassed at having forgotten about Billy Perkins' rather bumpy ride on the piece of converted fence gate. He thought for a moment, searching his memory for some novel idea he could boast having formulated in his own inventive mind. "Okay then, how about the chariot?"

"The chariot?" asked Finney. His disbelieving look

gave Jack a moment's pause to reconsider his recollection of that particular event.

"Okay, forget about the chariot!" Jack kicked himself for even mentioning the spectacle.

"Jack, as long as I'm left living on this earth, I don't believe I'll ever forget that one!"

It was after listening to Abe Lincoln read aloud from one of his history books about the Roman Empire that Jack gave birth to the ill-fated idea. It seemed innocent enough. He would simply take the large two-wheeled push cart Mr. Clary used for spreading fresh straw in the horse stalls, turn it backwards and tie it to ol' Henry, a large but very lazy mule belonging to Ignatius Bales. True, the creation lacked the splendor of a gold encrusted Roman chariot. And to get ol' Henry to move any faster than his usual slothful gate was nearly an impossible undertaking. But once complete, Jack proudly displayed his creation, much to the envy of the other kids who had gathered to witness his triumphal maiden-ride. He even wore a makeshift burlap tunic to imitate the Roman garment.

Now one thing can be said of young boys. Their eyes are easily blinded by the prospect of fame and admiration from their peers. Such was the reason Jack gave little consideration to how ol' Henry would react to having a Roman chariot attached to his harness. Expecting the old mule to barely skimp along, at the first crack of the whip Jack was hanging on for his very life! ol' Henry took off on a dead run, wildly jumping and kicking each step of the way. Amazingly, the makeshift chariot held together quite well as Jack bounced to and fro pulling with all his strength to rein the mule to a stop. It didn't work! The kids scattered in all directions in an effort to avoid being run over.

Within seconds, ol' Henry had exacted a terrible toll on the surroundings. Ignatius Bales' chicken coop was totally destroyed as the chariot's wheel caught the corner of the small containment. His chickens scattered frantically throughout the timber. In addition to not knowing that his mule was being used for such a purpose, it was said that he never did recover all of his fowl! If that wasn't enough, Mrs. Rutledge's prized perennial garden was literally destroyed, as was an entire length of fence separating the Rutledge's milk cows and Mentor Graham's sheep. But the worst happening was when ol' Henry set on a dead course for Hortense Plopper as she busied herself feeding the family pigs. Hortense was a big woman...really big! Weighing in at just over 400 pounds, she could barely lean over to drop the feed into the trough. Jack, still holding on with all his strength, tried to signal a warning but it was too late. With nowhere else to go to escape ol' Henry's approach, Hortense jumped backwards, breaking right through and splintering a split rail fence and landing face down in a mud puddle that only moments before contained half a dozen of the wallowing swine. Somehow Jack knew that the Roman Empire, at least the one of his own making, was about to abruptly fall.

"I seem to recall you having to feed the Ploppers' pigs and clean Ignatius Bales' mule stall for quite some time after that brilliant idea, Jack!" Finney seemed to be enjoying the moment.

"Yeah, well it wasn't my fault ol' Henry has such a bad sort of nature about him. How was I to know he'd kick up such a fuss?"

Finney continued to laugh as he stroked his oar

through the water. "Like I was saying Jack, you having a great idea is a stretch indeed!"

The sun was just beginning to drop below the horizon when the boys finally reached the area where the Salt Creek spills into the Sangamon. It was an area of relative flatness compared to the high cliffs encountered a few hours earlier. The Salt Creek was a narrower but deeper channel of water that merged with the Sangamon, and then wound its way westward to eventually empty into the much larger Illinois River. The Illinois River was a major waterway that provided a connecting route from Ft. Dearborn and the other northern settlements, westward to the mighty Mississippi near St. Louis. And while much river traffic could be seen daily at the spot where the Sangamon spilled into the Illinois, the spot where the Sangamon and Salt Creek merged, the very spot where the boys now sat floating in the slow current, was as remote a location as could be found anywhere.

The boys withdrew their oars from the water for a much needed rest. By the looks of the map, they were less than a half day from their destination. With their mouths watering for some of the plump catfish Finney had somehow managed to hook with the jerky, they decided the location would be an ideal spot to bed down for the night. It was flat enough that they could stay close to their canoe and not have to climb a steep bluff or rocky cliff to find a soft spot, while at the same time staying far enough away to escape the hoards of mosquitoes that infest the riverbank when the sun goes down.

As they paddled their canoe to the land's edge, the boys had no awareness that just out of sight and around the last bend the Redlegs too were busy pulling their canoe from the river. They had been quietly shadowing them since their departure, always careful to stay just out of sight. Being the experienced frontiersmen they were, the Redlegs had little difficulty stalking the boys as if they were hunting wild boar in the timber. The signs of their presence, things that would have been obvious to an experienced hunter—critters scattering in all directions and birds chirping nervously—went undetected by the boys.

Within a short time the moon had crawled to a spot high in the sky and cast an eerie light on the river and its surroundings. In the distance a lone coyote could be heard sounding its lonesome call. The boys' campsite was a simple one; a small fire, a few sticks to form a spit for cooking the catfish, and two bed rolls. As Jack sat under the night sky turning the catfish over the fire, an uneasiness set in. The ominous surroundings caused his thoughts to turn to the black curse. He wondered if they had yet entered the forbidden territory. The campfire caused shadows to dance across the trees. Each sound now caught his attention; the rustling of the leaves and bushes in the gentle evening breeze; a hoot owl keeping close watch over his nocturnal kingdom; a jackrabbit scurrying through the tall grass. As he stared into the crackling flame, his heart began to beat faster. He suddenly felt very alone, and for a brief moment wished he was back in his soft bed at Clary's Saloon.

"Whatcha thinking?" asked Finney, returning to the campsite after filling their canteens in the river. "You look like there's something mighty heavy on your mind."

"Finney?" began Jack, hesitantly. "If I was to tell you something I didn't tell you when I was telling you about the gold, you reckon you could find it in your heart to forgive me?" Jack knew he had to inform Finney of the danger lurking somewhere out there in the dark. He had to prepare him for the possibility of what lay ahead.

"Jack, what are you mumbling about?" Finney picked up a stick and poked the catfish. At that moment little else was on his mind but filling his hungry belly with a tasty morsel of the hardy fish.

"I was planning to tell you. I suppose I might just as well now." Jack took a deep breath. "Finney, have you ever heard tell of the black curse?"

"The black what?"

"The black curse. Abe says it lays in wait for anyone who comes into these parts looking for gold. He says no one who ever set out for it ever returned!"

"Abe said that, did he?" Finney did not appear convinced, or even much interested. A poke at the campfire sent burning ashes into the night sky. At that moment all he wanted to hear about was biting into the catfish.

"He surely did! He told me all about the creature just yesterday over a cup of sassafras."

"Well what's this creature supposed to look like?" asked Finney.

"I don't reckon anyone knows for sure." Jack peered nervously into the darkness beyond the fire's light. "No one who's ever seen it lived a day longer to tell the story!"

Finney pondered for a moment Jack's far-fetched tale. "It sounds more like one of Abe's yarns than a real curse." Another poke at the fire sent more ashes skyward. "Besides, why would a curse, no matter what kind of creature it is, care about gold anyway?"

"It's an injun curse," answered Jack. "See, Abe says

back when these parts belonged to the Kickapoo, they used gold to mold things for their spirit gods. And now, since the white man made these parts his own, well, you can figure the rest! It seems the spirit gods are none too happy these days." Jack waited in silence for Finney's response. He had to find a way to get him to take the creature seriously. To make their way into the forbidden territory without a healthy respect for the curse's power would be a disastrous venture.

"Injuns, you say?"

"Sure enough!" answered Jack. The gravity of their situation appeared to be sinking in as Finney's countenance suddenly changed.

"You know, come to mention it, my pa did tell me just a short time back about how injuns pray to spirit gods that look like wolves and such!"

"I'm afraid your pa had that one figured right," responded Jack. "Something tells me though this creature is much worse than a mere wolf!" The boys grew silent as they peered into the darkness around them. All was still but for the sound of the crackling fire. Its flame caused shadows to dance upon the trees around them. Neither gave any thought to turning the catfish that now shriveled on its stick. The sound of the owl hooting by the light of the moon only increased the eeriness of the moment.

It was true that when Illinois entered the Union of States in 1818, the Kickapoo occupied much of the central Illinois prairie, where they had lived since being forced from the Michigan territory to the north years earlier by the Iroquois tribes. They were mostly peaceful people who lived in villages and tilled the rich Illinois soil for their sustenance. And like most native bands, they worshipped many different deities, some strange composites of the various wild animals with whom they shared the wilderness. Following the War of 1812 however, white settlers came to the Illinois prairie in increasing numbers, and eventually forced the Kickapoo from their land, causing them to move south and west to the plains states and the Texas territory. It was not a migration looked upon with much favor by the Kickapoo, who viewed the white settlers as stealing away their fertile farm land and hunting grounds. It was said that as they departed central Illinois for their new homeland, the Kickapoo shaman placed a curse on the prairie soil that it would render the white man's seed infertile from that day forward.

"Maybe we should consider turning back?" Finney now had a nervousness in his voice. It was obvious he was ruling out any mischief on Abe's part in telling the story.

"We can't," responded Jack.

"What do you mean, we can't?" It was not the answer Finney was hoping to hear.

"I mean, we can't! We've come too far, and I'm not going back till I get my hands on that gold."

"But Jack," pleaded Finney. "What if that curse is as real as Abe says it is? It doesn't make much sense to sit around and wait for it to have its way with us!"

"Don't worry, I have a plan figured," said Jack. "You see, I'm guessing there's nothing worse for a curse than a good luck charm."

"A good luck charm?"

"Yup. That's why I made sure you brought along that lucky frog's leg you won from Jimmy Bales."

Finney's face suddenly took on a rather pale appearance. "But Jack..."

"Shhh...what was that?" The sound of cracking sticks in the distance startled the boys. They strained to see in the darkness the source of the noise.

"Levi, you IGNORAMUS!" whispered Coonrod. "How are we going keep an eye on those two varmints if you keep walking on them sticks? You sound like a herd of longhorn!"

"But Coonrod, the smell of them catfish has me so hungry I'm dizzy!" Levi licked his lips, and with his eyes closed slowly breathed in the aroma of the cooking catfish.

"Dizzy? You're not near as dizzy as you're going to get with my moccasin up side your scalp! Now keep your head low and your feet off them sticks!"

As the two Redlegs crouched low in the tall grass, they could see Jack and Finney in the distance peering nervously into the darkness. With the moon in front of them, and the light of the bright campfire too distant to have its effect, there was little chance of being spotted by the boys.

"What are you planning to do, Coonrod?" Levi's gaze was still fixed on the cooking catfish. At that moment he figured the best course to getting his hands on the sizzling mud bellies was to just shoot the boys. Little did he know the fish was quickly burning to a brittle on the spit because of the boys' inattention.

"We're not doing nothing."

"But Coonrod, why don't we just shoot them so we can get our map back?" Coonrod turned toward Levi with a silent but piercing sort of look. As he did, Levi sheepishly lowered his eyes to avoid contact. "That wasn't a good idea, was it?"

"Levi, you have never had a good idea! Why would

we shoot them boys when we've got gold to mine?"

Levi pondered the question momentarily. Then the confused look disappeared from his face. "Oh, I get it! We're going to capture them so they can dig the gold out for us!"

"Well I declare Levi," began Coonrod, with a toothless grin. "You finally used that brain God gave you to figure something right!"

Levi perked up with a proud demeanor. "It isn't so hard figuring these things in a proper way! Levi began to pick himself off the ground. As he did, the sound of the cracking sticks became louder.

"Levi!" yelled Coonrod, in a loud whisper. "What are you doing now?"

"I'm fixing to capture them boys like you said." Coonrod's reproving gaze caused Levi to sheepishly slump back into the tall grass. "I'm guessing that wasn't such a good idea either?"

"You guessed right, you IGNORAMUS!" Coonrod grabbed his coonskin hat and swatted Levi over the head. "Just what would we do with two squirming boys in the canoe? No siree. We'll just keep following them till we get to where we're going. Then we'll put the grabs on them."

About that time Levi's attention was diverted to a tree line just behind where they were crouched low in the grass. It sounded like heavy breathing. Levi strained to see in the darkness. It looked like a shadow of sorts. Then, with Coonrod continuing to keep an eye on the boys, the campfire cast off a sudden bright flicker of light, causing Levi to freeze in his place.

"C-C-Coonrod?" His voice trembled at what confronted him.

"What is it now?"

"Y-You reckon there's any g-g-griz in these parts?"

"Griz? Haven't you got a lick of sense? You know there's no grizzly this far to the east." Connrod continued to gaze at the boys, oblivious to the nervousness in Levi's voice.

"Then why's that mama griz staring at us like she's fixing to make stew of us?"

As Coonrod turned, less than a hundred feet away a large grizzly bear quietly stared at them, her large form dimly illuminated by the boys' campfire off in the distance.

"Oh lordy!" said Coonrod, as he too froze in his place.

"Coonrod, what does that mean when she shakes her head like she's doing right now?"

"Means she's fixing to attack," answered Coonrod, in a shaky voice.

"Does that mean we oughta do something?"

"Yup," answered Coonrod. "That means we oughta RUN! AGHHH!"

"AGHHH!"

"What is it?" asked Finney, in a frightened voice, as he and Jack strained to see through the darkness to discover the source of the noise. It was a terrifying combination of breaking branches, horrific growls, and loud shrieking screams!

"I don't know, but it sure sounds like it's heading straight for us!"

Finney's legs began to shake uncontrollably. "You reckon it's the c-c-curse?"

"I'd say the chances of that are better than good!" As the loud noise came even nearer, Jack bent over and picked up a large rock to prepare for the confrontation.

"What we going do?" asked Finney, his teeth now chattering loudly.

"I reckon there's only one thing to do," answered Jack, heaving the rock with all his strength in the direction of the approaching commotion. "RUN! AGHHH!"

Jack and Finney disappeared into the timber in a full sprint. Their yelling drowned out the sound of the Red-legs scurrying through the darkness with the growling bear snapping at their britches. Over hills, through creeks, and around trees the boys ran, each step of the way straining to see the evil that was behind them. At that moment there was no thought of gold! In the blackened darkness of night, well away from the campfire, the escape became more difficult. Every few steps one of the boys tripped over a log, ran into a low hanging tree branch, or felt his clothes ripped by thickets of thorny bushes. The noise behind them was at times indiscernible from their own loud commotion.

"I think we've lost it," said Finney, as they stopped finally to catch their breath. "I don't hear anything moving." The boys listened for any detectable sound. None but their own heavy breathing was apparent in the night's stillness. They were now a good distance from their campsite at the river's edge, and uncertain exactly how far their escape had taken them. There was no sight of the campfire's flickering shadows against any of the nearby trees.

"Did you lay eyes on it?" asked Jack, doubled over in an effort to relieve the sharp pain in his side. The knot on his head from a low-hanging branch had already started to swell.

"Can't say that I did," answered Finney, between breaths. "How about you?"

"Nope. I did hear some kind of screaming though when that rock I threw landed."

"Do you think you scared it away?"

"Surely not," answered Jack. "No human can scare away a curse! I'd say it was more than likely that lucky frog's leg of yours that had a part in driving it off. The creature must have felt it near!"

"But Jack..."

"No siree, doubt we'll see him again!"

"But Jack," persisted Finney.

"What?"

"I've been trying to tell you. My lucky frog's leg is sitting back beneath my pillow where I forgot it this morning. I was so concerned about getting out without Pa seeing me, I didn't even give it a thought!"

Jack's eyes opened wide as he slowly turned toward Finney. "Did I hear you right?"

"If you heard me say I don't have my lucky frog's leg anywhere near, then you heard me right!"

"Oh lordy!" said Jack, as he turned and gazed into the darkness. "That means that creature is more than likely still out there somewhere." The boys grew silent. Once again a lone owl could be heard hooting in the distance. The moon, now high in the sky, caused its own shadows to dance across the landscape, as a slight breeze ruffled the branches of the trees. "I got a bad feeling he's holed up out there just waiting to ambush us."

"What are we going do?" asked Finney.

"I reckon we best stay put until morning. Something tells me that creature probably can't stand much daylight. We should be safe then."

"What makes you think that?" Finney didn't sound so convinced.

"Because, I'm thinking whatever that creature is, it must have some wolf in him. And wolves don't like daylight. They're night hunters."

Finney just shook his head with a deep sigh, not sure what to make of Jack's theory. With fatigue beginning to set in, the boys quietly crawled beneath a large bush and gathered up enough leaves to form a pillow. In the distance the screech owl could still be heard singing its eerie call. A lone coyote joined in the chorus.

"Jack?" asked Finney.

"What?"

"When I fall off to sleep, would you grab hold of the biggest stick you can find and slug me right upside the head with it?"

"Whatever for?" asked Jack.

"For getting myself into a mess I knew better than to get myself in!"

Jack didn't respond. Now was not the time to convince Finney that the potential rewards of their adventure still outweighed the risks. True, the creature's presence this soon into their journey created a bit of an obstacle. Jack only hoped the morning sun would bring with it some bit of safety from the creature's deathly ways. Although the boys talked no further, except for an occasional "what was that?" it was near morning before either could shut his eyes and fall off to sleep.

5

THE FINAL LEG

The hot sun was already high in the sky when the boys finally picked themselves up from beneath the bush to make their way back to the campsite. Having gotten so few hours of real sleep, both felt a good amount of exhaustion as they labored their way back toward the river. Each step of the way was taken with great caution. Finney hoped Jack was right about the creature not wanting to show itself in the light of day. To reduce their odds of being attacked, they carefully navigated around any terrain shrouded in even the faintest of shadows. They purposed to trek their way back to the campsite in the wide-open and away from the trees. Figuring they had successfully outrun the creature once already, with a big enough head start perhaps they could again if the need presented itself.

Jack pondered the happenings of the previous night. Whatever it was that had chased them through the darkness had certainly gotten too close for comfort. The experience played over and over in his mind as he kept a vigilant watch of his surroundings. The image his imagination created of the creature's appearance was a horrible one. As quickly as the thought of being caught by its sharp claws popped into his mind, he repressed it with all his will. He couldn't believe Finney had forgotten his lucky frog's leg. He wondered if the creature would be shadowing them for the remainder of their trek to find the gold. It was not a pleasant thought to consider that the closer they got to the gold, the deeper they would be journeying into the forbidden territory. He already began to formulate a plan for locating a safe place to bed down when night fell again. The bush seemed to work well enough. He also reasoned that building a campfire, something normally done to keep critters away, was probably not a good idea with this particular critter.

It took only a few minutes for the boys to make their way back to the river and nervously approach the clearing where the campfire had burned the night before. From the looks of things it was quite apparent they had barely escaped a horrible end. The boys surveyed the area in disbelief. The few items they had carried up the embankment from the canoe—bedrolls, canteens, a few eating utensils—were now scattered about in all directions. Only a few bones remained of the plump catfish. Even the firewood appeared as if something had run right through the middle of it. A few smoldering embers were all that remained.

“Look at that, will you,” said Jack, pointing to the handmade spit, now lying in a broken heap a good distance from where it stood over the fire the night before. “The creature ate our catfish!”

“I reckon that’s better than the two of us being ate,” said Finney, with a nervous laugh. The boys quickly began to gather their belongings to make a hasty retreat to the canoe. As Finney walked toward a clump of berry bushes, he spotted something peculiar hanging from a sprout. “Hey Jack! Take a look at this.”

“Hmm...” Jack inspected the strange discovery. “It looks like the seat of someone’s britches!”

"You're not feeling a breeze, are you?" asked Finney, tilting his head to catch a glimpse of Jack's backside.

"Nope. How about you?"

"Not me," answered Finney.

"You don't reckon that creature wears britches, do you?"

"Not likely." Finney considered the find. "I'd say those are the remains of some other poor soul who passed this way! It doesn't look like he got as lucky as we did."

"It surely does seem that way," responded Jack. "Come on, unless we want someone to find our britches hanging from a bush someday, we better load up the canoe and head on downstream." The boys promptly gathered together the remaining items and made their way to the river's edge, making sure to keep a sharp eye for any movement in the surrounding bushes. Although the thought had crossed Jack's mind that perhaps the creature had destroyed the canoe to keep them from escaping, he breathed a sigh of relief to find it untouched and still sitting on the embankment where they left it the night before. With little delay they jumped in and set out on their way.

Once again, the current was barely noticeable as they floated away from the embankment. After rationing out the last of the beef jerky, the boys dipped their oars in the water and headed downstream. As they departed the area Jack kept a close eye on the embankment for any sign of the creature's presence. Each sound originating from the shoreline caused his head to turn in a panic. The boys wondered if the creature was quietly following them. Perhaps he was patiently laying in wait for the opportunity to attack? They each quietly wondered if such a beast could swim. By the looks of the map

Jack estimated they would come upon the fork in the river by mid-afternoon. The thought occurred to them to drop anchor and sleep in the canoe that night. Even if the creature could swim, the sound of his splashing would at least give them the opportunity to paddle away to safety before he could reach them and dispense his wrath, or so they hoped. As they pondered the idea, just out of sight around the last bend the canoe that had clandestinely shadowed them since their departure also set out in the lazy current.

"Ouch!" Coonrod slowly sat down on a pile of soft raccoon skins, but the pain in his bottom from being clawed by the mad grizzly bear was unbearable. He fidgeted back and forth searching for a comfortable position. None could be readily found.

"They say a good packing of cold mud will ease the pain a bit," said Levi, a white bandage covering the spot on his head where the large rock had found its mark.

"They say that, do they?"

"They sure do!"

"Levi, you IGNORAMUS!" yelled Coonrod, as he threw one of the coonskins at him. "How do you expect me to paddle this canoe with a packing of cold mud on my bottom side?"

"I guess I never gave it much thought, Coonrod."

"No, I guess you never did! Now get that paddle in the water so we can keep an eye on them two varmints! I don't want to lose sight of them."

With Coonrod in such a painful state, and Levi dizzy from being knocked on the head by the flying rock, paddling in the slow current quickly became a laborious task. To make matters even worse, having slept the night in a tree with the hungry grizzly bear laying patiently on the ground below now made it nearly impossible for either to set upright in the canoe. With each stroke of the oar both let out a muffled groan. An occasional growling belly signaled their unrequited hunger. Coonrod's anger toward the boys seemed to intensify each time his oar entered the water. He blamed them for his painful condition, and purposed to make their lives in the near future as unpleasant as his currently was.

With the happenings of the previous night now behind them, and with no further evidence of the creature's presence being apparent, Jack once again began to feel a tinge of excitement at the thought of finding the gold. His elation only intensified the closer they paddled to their destination. Just the thought of holding an arm load of the sparkling rock caused him to paddle faster and faster. Oh, what he could do with such a fortune! It was the type of auspicious circumstance a young boy dreamed of coming face to face with at some point in his life. Gold was after all the ultimate prize of all great adventures. On the frontier, whether mountains or prairie, it was talked about with wide-eyed wonderment. Many had spent their entire lives vainly searching for it. Many others had met their untimely demise in the process. It was said that the search for gold could cause a man to part company with his own sanity after a time, instilling in him a fever of sorts. Its allure was as powerful a force as any known.

"Finney?" asked Jack, after a long silence.

"Huh?"

"I was wondering, other than buying that new plow

for your pa, what are you figuring on doing with your share?"

"I'm not so sure there will even be a share!" answered Finney, continuing to stroke his oar through the water without glancing back at Jack in the rear of the canoe.

"Ah, come on. Just suppose we do find the gold, and lots of it, surely there's something you've got your heart set on?"

Finney tried to maintain his skeptical demeanor, but finally, as he began to ponder the idea of bringing back a canoe full of gold, he could hold back his smile no longer.

"Well?" continued Jack, trying to draw Finney into the discussion.

"Okay," he began, finally. "I reckon it would be nice to have the money to buy some things. I always wanted my own horse…maybe a stallion! Yeah, a white stallion…big and strong!" Finney pulled his oar from the water and drifted into his fantasy. "Of course, I couldn't have a white stallion without having one of those fancy saddles…the kind with gold studs all over it. Maybe even a shiny new flintlock to carry along when I ride him…one of those with the fancy engraving!"

"I declare," interrupted Jack. "For someone who's not so sure about finding the gold, it sounds like you've been thinking about how to spend it."

"I don't reckon it hurts to think."

"I reckon not," answered Jack. He smiled, knowing Finney was perhaps a bit more serious about their journey than he was letting on. It eased his guilt a bit for having convinced him to come along without being fully honest about the creature that had nearly had them in its grasp once already.

"And since we're on the subject anyway," continued Finney. "What are you planning to do with your share? Uh, that is if we find it, of course?"

"Oh, I haven't thought much about that part of it," answered Jack. The truth was he wanted to keep hidden his intentions to sway Becky Rutledge. He was at that paradoxical age when a young boy purposes to win over a young girl's affections with every conscious act, yet avoids at all costs ever admitting such a weakness of heart to another young warrior in search of courtship. "I reckon I'll just let Abe or Jack Kelso show me how best to spend it."

"Lordy!" said Finney. "Leave it up to Abe Lincoln and the only thing you'll ever get for your gold is a bunch of books!"

"That wouldn't be so bad. Abe says books are how a man gets to be great."

"He says that, does he?" asked Finney, with a snicker. "If I was to use that method of figuring, then I'd say Abe should be about the greatest man in the entire world by now. There's not another man, woman, or child in the village who reads as much as him!"

"It wasn't meant to be a joke!" snapped Jack. "Besides, if Abe would've won that politicing job he campaigned for, I'd say he'd be at least a smidgen great."

"How do you suppose Abe could ever win a politicing job? Pa says he can't even stock his store proper because he's off dreaming about things that don't matter much."

"I reckon they matter to him."

"I reckon so," answered Finney. "But if it takes reading that many books to make whatever matters to him matter, I don't reckon I ever want them same things to matter to me!" Jack just rolled his eyes at Finney's comment.

The truth was, throughout the village Abe Lincoln was known for his ability to waste away hours dreaming about things considered by most to be unimportant. If he wasn't somewhere beneath a shady tree reading a book of grammar or mathematics, chances were he was busy with a pencil and paper figuring a way to dredge the muddy Sangamon River for the steamers to make way. His belief in opening the river for greater navigation was so strong that he somehow managed to get his name on the ballot in the last election as a candidate for State Representative. He felt that with the power of the electorate behind him, getting the necessary money appropriated for the needed dredging would be a great deal more likely. Unfortunately though, with only four spots open and thirteen candidates vying for them, Abe managed to finish no better than a respectable sixth. The experience did wet his appetite though for political debate, and while most in the village considered him a bit unpolished to be a politician, he purposed to run again for public office at the earliest opportunity.

"Hey, look over yonder," yelled Jack. Off in the distance the boys could make out the unmistakable features of a fork in the river.

"You reckon that's Possum Creek?" asked Finney.

"It's got to be. The map doesn't show any other fork." As the boys paddled their canoe from the muddy Sangamon and into the mouth of the creek, a sense of excitement overcame them. Finding the small tributary where it appeared on the map gave them a sense that the gold might actually exist. At least the map wasn't just a product of someone's imagination. Whoever had sketched it had at least been this far. With each stroke of their oars the boys paddled faster. The black curse once again entered Jack's thoughts, but even that seemed an acceptable risk with visions of gold dancing before him. There was no turning back now. Curse or no curse, they were not stopping until they reached the spot on the map marking the location of the gold.

Once they had lost sight of the Sangamon River behind them, the boys quickly discovered that Possum Creek had even more bends and crooked fingers branching off in all directions. At one point Finney thought he caught sight of another canoe some distance back, but quickly dismissed it as just a passing trapper, odd though it was for such a remote area. The thought never occurred to him that these particular river travelers might have their sights set on the same gold he and Jack were journeying to claim as their own. He glanced a second time but the canoe had already passed out of sight around another bend. Before he could give it another thought his attention shifted to a more pressing problem. One thing that became quickly noticeable as they entered an area of the creek bounded by high rock formations on either side was that the current was beginning to move swifter and swifter. Suddenly, before either of the boys could recognize what lay before them, they rounded a sharp bend and found themselves trapped in a whitewater that sent their canoe wildly out of control.

"RAPIDS!" yelled Jack, as he made a futile effort to fight the current with his small oar. With a quick series of steep cascades the frothing whitewater intensified. Anything inside the canoe that was not tied down quickly spilled out as the small craft crashed into a protruding rock. Within seconds the rapids had turned the canoe backwards, with the boys fighting to hang on. There was little sense in trying to right the craft with their oars. The wild current was simply too strong. It was difficult to even discern which direction they were pointed in with the water crashing in on top of them. The water hit them with such force that it felt like they were being pelted with large rocks.

"JACK!" yelled Finney. "WE'RE COMING APART!" Before either realized it, they were in the water and struggling to swim free of the violent current, every few feet slamming into a rock or a piece of the canoe being thrown about by the rapids.

Now, in a frontier village such as New Salem was, there were certain lessons that a young boy had to learn if he desired to see adulthood. One of those lessons was how to swim in a whitewater. The secret is rather uncomplicated. You simply relax and allow the current to take you wherever it pleases until it runs its course. To fight it is hopeless, and ultimately will lead only to a paralyzing exhaustion.

Realizing their mistake, the boys discontinued their struggling and allowed themselves to float downstream. All around were the remnants of the canoe and its contents. The current thrashed them about and bounced them against protruding rocks and floating tree limbs. A full minute into their wild ride, having traveled a half mile from where the canoe crashed into the rocks, the boys finally reached calmer waters.

"You okay?" asked Jack, gasping for air as he lay on the wet sand.

"Other than swallowing half the creek, I reckon so," answered Finney, between breaths. "What now?"

The situation seemed hopeless as the boys sat wet

and dazed on the bank of the river. Their clothes were twisted in knots from tip to toe. The only things from the canoe that had managed to drift ashore with them were a few large pieces of the canoe itself. Worse yet, there didn't seem to be anywhere in sight a path leading from the shoreline to the top of the near vertical rock embankment.

"I don't rightly know," answered Jack, as he scanned the terrain around him. "I reckon the first thing we need to do is find a way out of here."

"How do you suppose we're going to get to the top of those rocks?" asked Finney, now shivering from his wild ride in the cold rapids.

Jack hesitated a moment. It certainly looked like a daunting task. A slight clearing a quarter mile downstream caught his attention. "It looks like there might be a path down yonder past that big rock in the water." The words had barely escaped his lips when the boys looked at each other with a sudden excitement in their eyes.

"That's it!" yelled Finney. "The big rock on the map!"

"It must be!" said Jack, as he stood up from the wet sand. "Come on!"

The boys ran through the shallow water as if the rock itself were a giant nugget of gold. Their wet and knotted clothes made it an exhausting challenge to run faster than a slow jog. As they reached the spot where the large piece of granite protruded from the water, Jack reached underneath his shirt and pulled out the buckskin map. "This is as far as the map goes. I reckon our gold is somewhere up there just waiting for us!"

"So where do we start?" asked Finney.

"First of all," began Jack, as he placed the map back inside his shirt. "We've got to get up this embankment. Then I suppose it's just a matter of looking. The old man must have marked it somehow."

Just past the rock formation the boys spotted an area of the embankment that appeared climbable. As they slowly and carefully made their way up the steep incline, some distance back, in the expanse where the rapids first announced their deadly intentions, the Redlegs were busy pulling their own canoe from the water.

"Coonrod, you figure they made it through?"

"Not unless they knew how to shoot a rapid. And I've never seen a young'n yet who knew how to shoot a rapid like this one!"

"How do you reckon we're ever going to find our map?" asked Levi.

"Well," began Coonrod, as he stared downstream. "If they did take a spill, and I'm figuring they did, then they more than likely washed up somewhere down yonder."

"But what if the map got lost in the rapids?"

"Levi, just once I wish you'd use that brain the good lord gave you! Don't you reckon them boys have taken a look at that map a time or two?"

"I suppose there's a chance of that."

"Well, there you go. We find those two varmints, we don't need the map. Instead, we'll just follow them right to the gold.

"You reckon the old man marked it somehow?" asked Levi.

"There's no doubt about that. Them boys likely won't

see it though when it's right in front of them."

"So what do we do?"

"When we see them stop and start nosing around in one area, that's when we'll grab them. After that we'll look for ourselves. It shouldn't be too much trouble to find once we're close to the spot."

Now being the experienced river traveler he was, Coonrod was able to spot the developing rapids long before he and Levi found themselves stuck tight in the current's grip. After pulling their canoe from the water and hiding it in a row of bushes, the Redlegs loaded their supplies and flintlock rifles on their backs and set out. Coonrod knew that most rapids run their course in less than half a mile. He expected to find the boys somewhere downstream without much of a walk. Quickly and quietly they climbed to the top of the rocky embankment and disappeared into the trees.

"Well?" asked Finney, as he and Jack sat on a log and wiped the sweat from their foreheads. It had been nearly two hours since they began searching the area atop the embankment where the large rock protruded from the creek below. By now their wet clothes had long dried as the hot midday sun bore down upon them.

"Well what?" asked Jack.

"Well, where's that strain of gold you said was bigger than a steamboat? The only thing I found was a bunch of dirt that's not worth sowing, and a strain of lime rock that wouldn't fetch a copper penny for the lot of it!"

"But it must be here," pleaded Jack. "This is where the map showed the X. We just have to keep looking."

"Keep looking? Need I remind you Jack, we've got

no food, no way to catch any, and no canoe to get back home in! No siree, the only thing I'm looking for is a clear path back to New Salem!" Finney stood from his seat on the log and brushed himself off. "Now, are you coming along, or are you going to sit there on that log dreaming about something that probably doesn't even exist?"

Jack sat on the log and considered Finney's comments. Maybe he was right? Perhaps the map was only someone's clever tool to swindle a hefty premium from some soul blinded by the prospect of gold? He began to wonder if their journey was nothing more than a futile effort to chase down something that existed only in someone's imagination. He also considered what would happen if they returned empty-handed. Aside from losing all hope of ever courting Becky Rutledge, there was little doubt that Mr. Clary would work him at a ruthless pace for a good long time for getting his best canoe destroyed beyond use. To return without the gold was certainly a bleak alternative. All things considered, Jack decided there was little to lose in continuing the seemingly pointless search.

"I'm staying," he began. "I've come too far to turn back now. That gold is here somewhere, and I'm not quitting until I lay my hands on it!"

"Suit yourself," said Finney, as he turned and began his long trek back to New Salem. As he walked away, he listened for any movement on Jack's part, hoping Jack would join him for the long return trip. There was none detected. "But don't say I never told you...AGH!"

To his amazement, Jack looked up to find Finney nowhere in sight. "Finney? Finney?" There was no sign of him anywhere. "Come on now, don't be playing no games!" With the happenings of the previous night still fresh in his mind, Jack nervously jumped to his feet and prepared to race for the river at the slightest sign of the creature's presence. He suddenly had the frightening suspicion that they had been stalked to their present location.

"Jack, I'm down here!" Jack could not believe his eyes as he followed the voice to find Finney at the bottom of a large hole situated at the base of a high rock formation. The weathered boards and brush that had hidden its opening now lay in a heap on top of him.

"Finney, what are you doing in that hole?"

"I'm not here because I want to be!" The hole was too deep for Finney to climb out, and the makeshift ladder that previously stood upright inside the hole had busted to pieces when he fell right on top of its fragile frame. Finney considered his predicament. "Maybe if we tie our belts together it might reach far enough so I can grab hold?"

"I suppose it's worth a try." Jack removed his rope belt and leaned over the edge of the hole to catch Finney's as he threw it up. As he did, his eyes caught a most unbelievable sight that nearly took his breath away. There below him, illuminated by a single ray of bright sunlight, was a wall of sparkling gold rock!

"Finney, look!"

Finney's lower jaw dropped as he turned to see the shiny wall behind him. "Lordy, Jack! I think we just found the mother lode!"

"YAHOO!" yelled Jack. "AGH!" Before he knew it, he too found himself momentarily dazed and sitting at the bottom of the hole on top of Finney and the heap of broken boards.

"What's the idea?" yelled Finney. "You didn't need to jump in on top of me!"

"I didn't jump," answered Jack. "I got pushed!"

"Pushed? Now who could've pushed you out here in the middle of nowhere?" asked Finney, as he picked himself up off the cold ground.

"We coulda," came a voice from atop the hole. The boys looked up to see the two smiling Redlegs peering in.

"Jack," began Finney, in a slow voice. "I'm surely hoping that ain't who I think it is?"

"I'm afraid it is," answered Jack, nervously. Suddenly, with Coonrod and Levi's loud laughter exposing their toothless grins, the sparkling wall of gold left their thoughts as quickly as it had entered.

6

CAPTURED!

"What do you think they're doing up there?" asked Jack, as he jumped up and down trying hard to get a better look outside the hole. Even a healthy leap brought him no closer than six feet from the top of his outstretched hand to the opening above. It had been nearly an hour since they had fallen captive to the Redlegs. They could hear them moving about setting up a campsite, but could not clearly make out their words. Their imprisonment caused an uneasy feeling to set in. So far no part of their journey had gone according to plan, and now it was about to get even worse. To be stuck in a hole and at the complete mercy of two savage frontiersmen, such as the Redlegs undoubtedly were, was not an ideal situation to be in, no matter how you looked at it.

"Why's it matter what they're doing?" answered Finney, sitting with his back against the wall of gold and staring into the cold ground. "Whatever it is, the two of us are still stuck in this hole."

"I don't reckon it hurts to know." Jack noticed the dejected look on Finney's face. He began to feel a sense of guilt. After all, it was his adventure; his crazy idea to set out in search of gold using a dead man's map, all the while knowing that men of such savage repute as the Redlegs might happen onto their plan. Considering their predicament, Jack formed the opinion that the gold probably wasn't as important to Finney as it was to him. After all, Finney didn't seem to have any trouble attracting the affections of the young ladies in the village. That was apparent by the large number of hearts carved into the oak tree containing his name. He also didn't seem to want for much. Finney's father was a successful blacksmith, and made a comfortable living fashioning horseshoes, kitchen utensils, tools, and other implements for the villagers. Seldom did the wagon arrive from Springfield without a piece of fine furniture, new clothes, or a can of premium tobacco loaded on board and destined for the Reeves' cabin. So for Finney, maybe it was more than just the gold that motivated him? The thought crossed Jack's mind that perhaps it was a sense of loyalty to their friendship that caused him to come along on the journey. After a long silence his need to confess his guilt got the better of him.

"It looks like I got us in a fine mess this time, huh?"

"It looks you did for sure!" snapped Finney. Without looking up, he tossed a small rock against the opposite wall of the pit. He took no notice of the sparkling ore embedded in the stone. At that moment it was the furthest thing from his mind.

"Well, if it makes any difference to you, I'm sorry. I didn't know they were following us." Jack took on a somber look. His embarrassment over their present circumstance was apparent. From the corner of his eye Finney noticed the change in Jack's countenance. Now being the best friends they were, neither had a habit of staying angry at the other for any duration. It just didn't seem to accomplish much in the long run. Finney warmed a bit to Jack's downtrodden demeanor.

"Ah, forget about it." Finney raised his head with a

smile. "I don't recollect anyone tying me in that canoe to get me here."

"Yeah, I reckon not!" said Jack, with a smile. He felt relieved to know Finney held no bad feelings toward him. Given the predicament they were in, he found comfort and a sense of strength in their friendship. It was a bond that would have to be relied on heavily to get themselves free of the hole and out of the clutches of the Redlegs. Together they had overcome seemingly insurmountable obstacles in the past. This wouldn't be the first time they would have to combine their wits to extricate themselves from some hopeless mess. The truth was, they had become quite proficient at it. Although Jack had a certain talent for getting them in a quagmire such as they presently found themselves, it was his sense of daring and adventure, no matter how great the odds against him, coupled with Finney's level-headed manner and knack for reasoning through even the most difficult of problems, that truly made for an effective combination. Together they worked like a well-oiled steam engine, the talents of one complimenting those of the other. The resourcefulness of their partnership was well known throughout the village, especially among those who at various times found themselves victim to their inventive ways. Certainly no one was better acquainted than their school teacher, Mentor Graham. In the classroom, it was a constant endeavor for Mr. Graham to maintain some sense of order, and a constant challenge for Jack and Finney to disrupt it! Their methods were not easily detected, and Mr. Graham always kept a sharp eye for the least bit of evidence that a plan was being hatched. He had become quite proficient at it. However there was one problem. The better he got, the more proficient Jack and Finney became at avoiding detection. It was like the sword play of two dueling buccaneers, each circling the other and waiting for just the right moment to lunge forward and exact the winning blow on his opponent!

Now the problem with acquiring a reputation such as the boys had is that it becomes like a double-edged sword. On the one hand the boys were quite proud of their ability to attract Mentor Graham's paranoid-like suspicions, and routinely boasted of such to their classmates. On the other hand though, they unavoidably became the primary suspects in almost every disruptive occurrence in the classroom, regardless of who the true perpetrator was. From time to time some other young jokester with a mischievous nature would even attempt to exploit the boys' reputation by quietly allowing the blame for his own disruptive scheme to fall upon them. Jack and Finney had on more than one occasion felt Mr. Graham's hickory stick across their bottoms for someone else's wrongful ways! It was the price they paid for having reputations in constant conflict with Mr. Graham's intentions.

After a few moments of silence Finney spoke. "Jack? What do you think they're going to do with us?" The uncertainty was apparent in his voice.

"I've been trying to figure that one out since we wound up in this hole," answered Jack. "I can't say that I have much of an answer yet."

"I'll tell you what we're going to do!" came a loud voice from above, as a pick dropped to the bottom of the hole along with a pile of long, skinny burlap bags; the kind normally used for beans and cornmeal. "If you two young'ns don't get busy digging out that gold, me and Levi here are going to fill both your hides full of lead! Now start digging!"

From the sound of Coonrod's voice it was obvious to the boys that their predicament was no practical joke. No toothless grins were apparent as the Redlegs peered in through the top of the hole. At that moment their situation seemed quite hopeless. All the excitement they had felt at the prospect of finding the gold now suddenly evaporated. Little thought was even given to the wall of sparkling rock only inches from where they stood.

"Mister?" began Jack, in a nervous tone. "We've never dug for gold before. I don't reckon we much know how." Jack had little hope that his plea would actually convince the Redlegs to release them. He figured he had nothing to lose by trying.

"Well then, I'll tell you how," began Coonrod, impatiently. "One of you take hold of that pick and get to digging the gold out of that there rock, and the other'n one bag it up! Now that don't sound too difficult, does it?"

"I reckon not," answered Jack. He turned and gazed at the wall of rock. With all the excitement over the gold having now waned, the idea of digging it out was not a welcomed thought.

"Then get busy!" yelled Coonrod. "And the first one I catch sitting on his backside will be sorry he did!"

With the thought that the mess they were in was his fault, Jack grabbed the pick and began the difficult task of digging the gold ore out of the wall of solid rock. With each strike of the pick's sharp point only a few slivers managed to break free. A quick calculation in his head and he reasoned it would take days to complete their task. It would have been one thing to return home from their unannounced absence with a canoe full of gold, but to return empty handed was not an option Jack much wanted to consider, especially in light of having destroyed Mr. Clary's best canoe in the manner they did. In a pioneer village, a good canoe, the kind made of birch bark, was not an easy thing to come by. Only a few craftsmen within a day's ride of the village were known to possess the skills needed to build a truly river-worthy vessel. Given the cost to procure a good canoe, most men protected their investment with great vigilance.

While he labored away at the demanding chore, Jack contemplated the situation they were in. He tried to make some sense of the happenings, and wondered how they had made it this far without detecting the two Redlegs shadowing them. He thought back to when he first came face to face with the Redlegs at Abe's store. He was now certain they had seen through his unconvincing efforts to avoid their inquiry. He wondered what they had in store for them once the gold was all mined. Would they let them out of the hole? Maybe they were planning to simply leave them there once they had their canoe loaded with the freshly mined gold and journeyed on? Jack glanced toward the sky and imagined buzzards circling about. Just the thought of it caused his mouth to go dry.

The chips and slivers of gold began to pile on the ground as Finney nervously filled one of the small burlap bags. He too silently contemplated their situation. He wondered about his family and what they were doing at that moment. He figured his father was no doubt waiting patiently for his return in order to dispense his discipline. If only he knew about their present dilemma, Finney thought. Suddenly the idea of getting his backside set ablaze didn't seem such a bad thing. At that moment he even felt a tinge of appreciation for his father's rather harsh method. Perhaps if he had appreciated it a bit more when Jack dreamed up his grandiose plan he wouldn't be in the mess he now found himself. As he tied the bag shut and stacked it on the opposite side of the hole from where Jack busied himself with the pick, he gazed upward through the opening at the bright blue sky above. He wished he were in some other place, preferably back in the village chasing the likes of Sally Armstrong rather than bagging the precious rock that had now landed them in their granite prison. He was relieved to see that the Redlegs were no longer peering in at them.

"Psst...hey Jack, they're gone."

"They're up there somewhere," answered Jack, stopping to wipe the sweat from his brow with the sleeve of his shirt. "Unless you want a backside full of buckshot, I'd suggest you keep filling them bags."

Finney continued to keep his eye on the hole's opening while he filled a second bag with the gold slivers. "Jack, we've got to get out of here! Who knows what them Redlegs have in mind for us!"

"I know," answered Jack. He continued to half-heartedly strike the pick against the rock wall in order to avoid attracting the Redlegs' suspicion. "I've been trying to figure us a plan."

"Well I surely do hope you figured a good one."

"As a matter of fact, I have," answered Jack. "But first we have to wait till dark."

"Why wait till then?"

"You'll see. Right now we need to keep digging before they catch us standing around doing nothing."

The boys grew quiet as they returned to the drudgery

of digging out and bagging up the sparkling ore. With the afternoon sun now bearing down on them, the hole was fast becoming hotter than a smoke house. Again, Jack glanced upward at the imaginary buzzards, but the blinding light of the sun caused him to quickly look away. He continued to strike the pick unceasingly against the rock wall to avoid the Redlegs' wrath. Wherever they were, he felt certain they were within earshot. Any prolonged silence would surely attract their unwanted attention. With the beginnings of a plan swirling around in his thoughts, he figured it best to leave the impression they were complying with the orders they had been harshly given.

As Jack soon discovered, one can strike a heavy iron pick against solid rock only for so long before it becomes an extremely arduous task. To worsen matters, only a small indentation had thus far been made in the wall of the pit. His lack of progress was demoralizing, and only intensified his fatigue. Within an hour his exhausted arms could swing no more.

"Jack," whispered Finney, seeing his increasing distress. "Trade me places!"

"I reckon that would be just fine," answered Jack, dropping the pick where he stood. "How many bags have we filled?"

"Looks like nearly ten," answered Finney, taking a quick count.

"That's all? It feels like we've dug out at least fifty bags worth!" Jack dropped to the ground in complete exhaustion. He gazed at the small number of bags stacked neatly against the opposite side of the hole. His frustration was apparent.

"A lot of what you dug out is rock with no gold in it," said Finney. "I figured they would skin us alive if we bagged it up."

"I suppose you're right." Jack picked up an empty bag and began to fill it with the slivers and chunks that lay scattered about the ground around them. As he did, Finney took to striking the pick against the wall. With his first strike against the hard rock a pain shot up his arm and throughout his entire body. His muffled groan caught Jack's attention.

"Don't worry," began Jack, the exhaustion still apparent in his voice. "After a short time you won't feel it anymore."

Finney held his arm waiting for the pain to subside. "Well now," he began. "That's a reassuring thought." In a moment he was back to his task. As he labored away his mind wandered, searching for a way out of the mess they were in. There had to be some way of escaping the hole. In his mind he calculated the distance to the hole's opening above. By his figuring, even standing on each other's shoulders would still leave them a good two feet short. Another idea came presently to mind.

"Jack?" he began, continuing to strike the rock just hard enough to make a noise in case the Redlegs were nearby. "Do you reckon we could tunnel our way out of here?"

"Tunnel?"

"Yeah, like the time we dug up under Lucy Bales' house."

Jack stopped his activity and inspected the wall of rock. "Finney," he answered. "I reckon we'd be old men by the time we dug our way through this rock. 'Besides, if the time we dug up under Lucy Bales' house is any measure, I'd say we weren't the best tunnel diggers anyway."

"Yeah, I reckon you're right," said Finney, as a smile cracked his lips. Even as exhausted as he was, the incident still humored him. "Jack, I have never seen a look on a person's face like I did on yours that day!"

Jack too was momentarily amused at his recollection of the event. "It was mighty funny indeed." For the present time both of the boys seemed to set aside any thought of their predicament.

Lucy Bales was New Salem's biggest flirt. She had blond hair, blue eyes, and a smile that could attract a young boy's passion like a half-eaten watermelon attracts flies! She was one of those girls who was well aware of her beauty and never missed an opportunity to lead on an admiring young lad like a billy goat on a leash. She was a master of her art. More than who cared to admit it had been lulled by her hypnotic ways into believing they had gained her affections, only to be tossed aside like a worn rag when her self-serving motives no longer required her feigned interest. She was cold and calculating in her method, and in a strange sort of way this quality only intensified her mystique among the boys of the village.

"You have to admit, Jack," said Finney, his smile still stretched across his tired face. "Had it worked, it would have been worth all the trouble we went to!"

"There's no doubting it!" answered Jack, returning the smile and thinking back to their rather ambitious plan. For all her superficial toying around, from time to time Lucy Bales did discover in her heart a sincere fondness for some young lad. Unfortunately though, she had one other circumstance about her that made it next to impossible for some young Romeo to fulfill his desires by holding her hand or feeling her finely sculpted lips press against his cheek; she had a mother who routinely grabbed the hair and ears of any unsuspecting lad who attempted to gain favor with her precious daughter.

Mrs. Bales was one of those women who struck fear in the hearts of young boys. She was bigger than an oak tree and had a mustache thicker than most men. Among the adults she was rumored to be a descendant of some great and mighty warlord. Few ever crossed her path unnecessarily. Her intimidating way caused even the men around the village to shudder in her presence. Being a strong and faithful Lutheran, she was strictly against the practice of consuming intoxicating drink, and with her thick German accent would routinely chastise those who did. Few would dare to venture forth from Clary's Saloon when she passed by on her daily trek to the church. Most would lower their boisterous voices to avoid detection and a later tongue lashing on the virtues of sobriety. Whether she was shouting "Amen!" to one of Reverend Cartwright's Sunday sermons, or outside tilling a garden, Mrs. Bales' King James Bible was always close at hand.

It was during one of those days when the fish weren't biting when Jack, Finney, and 'Mud' Armstrong devised a plan to skirt Mrs. Bales' impenetrable barrier to her daughter. Their plan seemed uncomplicated enough. They would simply dig a tunnel underneath the Bales' cabin and come up directly beneath Lucy's bedroom. It would then be a simple matter of waiting for Lucy to make her nightly trek to her bedroom to change into her nightclothes for bed. If their plan worked, not only would they watch the entire drama through the cracks in Lucy's floor, but they would maintain the tunnel to relive the experience nightly. Mud even had the ingenious idea of charging other kids for the experience. They estimated they could earn a small fortune within days of announcing the venture. Given Lucy's propensity for luring young boys like a worm beckons a hungry catfish, the thought crossed their minds that perhaps she would even agree to willingly participate in the scheme for a share of the profits. Of course no thought was given to the fact that few kids in the village ever had any money to spend in such a manner. Furthermore, they quickly reasoned that such an arrangement would only lead to their plan being discovered by some suspicious parent livid at the thought of their son not being able to account for a hard-earned nickel or dime originally intended for the Sunday collection.

Working under cover of darkness, the boys labored for nearly a week digging the short distance from an embankment just behind a row of bushes to their destination beneath Lucy's floor less than twenty feet away. To hide their devious plan they simply scattered the freshly excavated dirt each night in a nearby garden and covered the hole with a piece of cut brush. They even took precautions to reinforce the small tunnel with the remnants of an old split rail fence. It was truly the perfect plan.

The work was exhausting, but finally, with their hands sore and blistered, the boys reached their objective. It was Jack who broke through the dirt to feel the wooden floor planks no more than six inches above the ground. Mud had actually been inside the Bales' cabin on occasion, so it was left up to him to guide the tunnel to the right spot beneath Lucy's bedroom. After digging out enough room for all three of them to squeeze close enough to the floor to press their faces against the wooden planks, their plan was ready to be implemented. Finney even managed to bring along a small chisel and hammer to prepare for the anticipated event by quietly knocking a knot out of one of the floor planks to provide for better viewing. It was not uncommon to find such holes in many of the cabin floors around the village. The boys were certain they could pull off the feat without raising Lucy's suspicions.

The moon was high in the sky by the time the boys had taken their spot beneath the cabin floor. With each passing minute their excitement compounded. This was it, the moment for which they had labored. Fortunately, as they popped their heads up underneath the floor, Lucy's bedroom was dark and empty. Mud was so excited that he ran the top of his head into the wooden planks, causing a loud 'thump' to sound throughout the room. As he nursed the sore spot on his head, Finney quickly forced a knot from one of the pine planks as the others peered in through the gaping cracks. Then within minutes of their arrival at the tunnel's end the blessed moment arrived.

Hearing Lucy open the door and enter the darkened room was enough by itself to drive the boys to an excited frenzy, but when they heard the unmistakable sound of her clothes hitting the floor, Mud's teeth began to chatter uncontrollably! As Lucy fumbled with the oil lamp the boys fidgeted to and fro to better position themselves to view the event. It was better than they had hoped for. With the striking of a single match they were about to see the object of their passions fully de-clothed and in the fullness of her glory! Jack considered at that moment that perhaps God's favor was shining down upon them in their noble quest. Of course he also considered that Reverend Cartwright would likely disagree with that assessment.

Now it seems that young boys, especially Mud Armstrong, have a knack for miscalculating time, distance, and direction. When the match was struck, with the boys each straining to catch a glimpse of the heavenly sight above them, there stood Mrs. Bales, naked as a chicken in a Dutch oven! In a short moment their excitement gave way to shock as they took in the indescribable sight. Then, as if the humor of the spectacle hit each of them at once, the boys were fighting to hold back their laughter. They motioned to each other to quickly back out of the tunnel, each of them biting their tongues to avoid detection. Jack was the first to let go a loud cackle. He simply could hold it no longer. They froze in place while Finney held his hand tightly over Jack's mouth, hoping to quell his uncontrollable urge to laugh.

Once Mrs. Bales started pouring hot water through the cracks in the floor at what she thought were raccoons, the boys exited the tunnel even quicker than they had entered it! Any need for stealth quickly faded with the scalding water pouring in on top of them. Suddenly the situation seemed void of humor. Making matters worse, Mrs. Bales continued her pursuit all the way to the edge of the room, pouring hot water through the cracks with each step. There was no escaping it in the tight quarters of the tunnel.

It would be the last time the boys would ever journey to the underside of Lucy Bales' cabin. If the risk of coming face to face with Mrs. Bales wasn't enough to keep them from again carrying out their plan by rerouting the tunnel, in the end it really didn't matter. With the first heavy rain the narrow passageway collapsed and quickly filled in, hiding for all eternity any remnant of their ill-fated scheme. Mr. Bales blamed the sudden dimple in his yard on a family of moles. It was just as well, the boys decided. There was little doubt the tunnel would eventually have been discovered. Jack reconsidered any part God may have had in the plan. One thing was for certain, it would be the last time they would trust Mud Armstrong for directions.

"Jack?" began Finney. "If we can't tunnel our way out of this hole, how are we going to get out?"

"Like I was saying," answered Jack. "I have a plan figured."

Finney contemplated his confident tone. "Jack, I'm reminded that it was a plan of yours that got us in here in the first place. I surely do hope this one's a bit more successful."

"That I can't promise," answered Jack. "But unless you think otherwise, I'm figuring just about anything is worth a try."

"Yeah, you have a point there," answered Finney. "So what's your plan?"

About that time the boys could make out the sound of approaching voices. "I'll tell you later," whispered Jack. "We have to wait till them Redlegs fall off to sleep. Right now we best keep digging." No sooner had the boys returned to their chore when the Redlegs peered in through the top of the hole.

"It seems to me I should be hearing more of that pick striking against that rock," began Coonrod in a calm voice.

"We're working real hard, mister," answered Jack, deceived by Coonrod's present demeanor. "I'm thinking we could work a bit harder though if you were to throw down some of that food I smell up on the cook fire. We're mighty hungry from digging out all this gold."

"Hungry, are you?" asked Levi with a devious sort of grin. "Maybe you would like a piece of that tasty venison we got turning on the spit?"

The boys nodded in affirmation, their mouths watering at the thought of biting into a piece of the freshly cooked meat. They hadn't eaten since earlier in the day when they finished off the remaining jerky.

"What do you think, Coonrod?" continued Levi. "You reckon we ought to share our dinner with these two varmints?"

"Well now," answered Coonrod, his voice still calm. "I think sharing with these hard working lads is a fine idea indeed. In fact, I believe what I'm fixing to share with them...IS A LOAD OF BUCKSHOT IF THEY DON'T GET OFF THEIR LAZY BACKSIDES AND GET TO MINING THAT GOLD QUICKER!"

The sudden change in Coonrod's voice startled the boys back to work. Finney fumbled with the pick and quickly returned to striking the rock wall. Jack did likewise, bagging up the slivers and chips of rock that flew in all directions with each strike of the pick. Nothing further was said. The message was clear. No venison would be coming their way. For now they would have to fight their hunger by not thinking about food. This was made more difficult by the mouth-watering aroma that now wafted through the air around them. As the Redlegs returned to their campsite, no doubt preparing to feast on the tasty venison, the boys again grew quiet and busied themselves with the painstaking task of digging out and bagging up the sparkling ore. Soon night would fall, and Jack's plan could be put into action. In the boys' minds it could not be soon enough!

7

AN ESCAPE PLAN

As hard as he tried to stay awake, Jack's eyes became increasingly heavy from the day's exhausting work. The full moon was now visible in an ominous way through the top of the hole. In the dark of night, with a slight mist hanging in the air, the cold earth caused him to tremble. All was silent in the area where the Redlegs were bedded down by the campfire. At that moment Jack wished he too were lying next to the fire enjoying the comfort of its warmth. His mind wandered as he slipped into that state between sleep and awake when it becomes difficult to discern which is which. As his thoughts suddenly were swallowed up by dreamful visions like a catfish quaffing a hardy worm, he found himself back in the village preparing to drop a hook and line in the muddy Sangamon with Slicky Bill.

As he did with his friend Abe Lincoln, Jack looked up to Slicky Bill like a big brother. And while Abe took it upon himself to teach Jack the kinds of things of greater import to more learned men, Slicky Bill passed along to Jack's learning the more practical tips, methods, and secrets of life; things like knot tying, beaver trapping, and navigating by the stars. Of course, Slicky Bill also had a penchant for teaching things better left untaught to a young boy with a mischievous tendency. Jack once spent a full three days in bed, his stomach cramping and convulsing in pain, after learning and putting into practice the proper method for chewing and spitting a chaw of tobacco. A single swallow of the thick pungent juice was enough to convince Jack to never again try such a thing. Slicky Bill said he had never personally seen a person turn so green about the gills! Of course, the event was just one among many that caused the ladies of the village to form a rather low opinion of Slicky Bill and his ways.

One particular talent Slicky Bill taught Jack to the point of perfection was the art of poker. Now this wasn't simply the ability to play a good game of Stud or Blackjack. No, Jack's talent was helping Slicky Bill beat the pants off the frontiersmen who routinely passed through the village on their way to the western territories. Most who made their way westward through the village would invariably find their way to Clary's Saloon. And when they did, without fail Slicky Bill would conveniently show up with a deck of cards and an itching to gamble. It really had little to do with beating any sort of odds. In reality, Jack and Slicky Bill had developed a complex system of signals for Jack to tip Slicky Bill to his opponent's hand. During the game Jack, who would always wander in rather inconspicuously a few minutes after Slicky Bill to avoid any suspicion, would act the part of a disinterested spectator and attempt to position himself in view of the unsuspecting opponent's hand. It was then simply a matter of placing his hands, arms, hat, or even the part in his blonde hair, in the appropriate position to signal the hand to Slicky Bill.

Now this method was effective for Jack and Slicky Bill in almost every circumstance but one; when the person being cheated was even more proficient in the art of cheating than they were. Such was the case one ill-fated day when a certain shyster familiar with Jack and Slicky Bill's method happened into Clary's Saloon. It took little prodding on the part of Slicky Bill to engage the stranger in a game of stud poker. Given the fact the stranger was unsure how to even properly place a wager, Slicky Bill was confident that picking him clean of his currency would be easier than stealing candy from a child. Of course Slicky Bill failed to recognize the true nature of the stranger's convincing performance, or his reasons for offering Jack a seat close by and in full view of his hand.

Because he was guaranteed to win, given his dishonest method, Slicky Bill seldom brought money of his own earning to the table. Instead, he would flash a roll of money to his opponent that in reality was just two one-dollar bills with a wad of plain paper in between. In order to engage an opponent it was important to demonstrate that he actually had a sizable amount of money to wager and possibly lose. Besides, to enter such a competition with little or no money instantly marked the player as one who intended to win in a dishonest manner. And on the frontier, wild as it was, to cheat a man out of his hard-earned money was a certain way for one to earn his eternal reward in a quick manner.

After the first couple hands, with Jack flashing his subtle signals with great proficiency, Slicky Bill began to consider that perhaps one of his biggest takes ever was at hand. The stranger seemed to enjoy losing! He even made it easy for Jack by holding his hand in plain view. Of course what Slicky Bill and Jack didn't know was that the stranger had a handful of aces, kings, and even a few queens strategically placed in his shirt sleeves, his cuffs, and even under his hat. After lulling Slicky Bill with his performance he set the trap by wagering more cash than Slicky Bill had, either on the table or in his pocket. After receiving the signal from Jack that the stranger had nothing larger than two fives, a hand easily beaten by Slicky Bill's two jacks, he confidently matched the wager by placing the bogus roll of bills at the center of the table.

Jack was so excited at the prospect of winning a large pot that he took no notice of the stranger's sleight of hand, exchanging his entire set of cards for a full house of aces and kings. Slicky Bill could not believe his eyes when he turned them over with a devious grin. Of course, now his problem quickly became the fake roll of money sitting on the table, and its close proximity to the pair of pistols strapped to the man's waist. On the frontier there were certain unwritten rules among poker players. One was that it was entirely acceptable to shoot a man who did not follow through on a wager. Another was that it was perfectly within a man's Biblical right to do the same to a cheater, only with a lot less argument or thought! Something at that moment told Slicky Bill the stranger was no novice. He had been taken by a true professional. He also reasoned that the stranger probably knew the money was not real, and would more than likely negotiate for something in its place; likely his true motive all along.

Slicky Bill lost his best horse that day. It was a heavy price to pay for his less than honest ways. Reverend Cartwright would have called it God's judgment; the wages of sin! For having played a part in the failed scheme, the stranger made Jack hoist up and tie down a load of supplies to the back of his newly acquired steed. As he slowly meandered his way down the road leading from the village, the horse's bridle in hand and a smile on his face, both Jack and Slicky Bill pledged at that moment to never again attempt such a risky pretense. Any fair amount of money was hard enough to come by on the frontier, but a good horse was truly a prized commodity. It would be nearly a month before Slicky Bill had successfully swindled enough travelers out of their cash to purchase another.

The sound of the wind rustling through the trees startled Jack awake just as he was preparing to slip off into a deep sleep. He struggled to open his eyes and think coherently. It was not an easy task from the bottom of a cold dark hole. The cool breeze against his face helped him escape his slumber. He knew it was now or never. They had to make their flight from the hole while the idea was fresh in their minds, and before more of the exhausting labor got the better of them. Once free of their captors, perhaps then they could formulate a plan to reclaim the gold. But for now the precious rock would have to be relegated to a secondary consideration. Besides, Jack was quite certain Finney had by now lost all interest in the sparkling ore. He reasoned that to even suggest they consider the gold a factor in devising a plan to get as much distance as possible between them and the Redlegs would not be a very constructive proposition at this juncture.

As he gazed up through the top of the hole at the full moon reaching its apex in the night sky, the black curse, which had somehow escaped his thoughts, came presently to mind. Had the creature followed them to their location? If it had, why had it not attacked the two Redlegs? Perhaps it hadn't yet reached the bluff that now held them prisoner in its rocky underground? For now, he decided that an escape into the darkness would be a risk worth taking. Besides, if the creature were moving in their direction, to wait any longer, especially confined to the hole, would guarantee he and Finney quickly becoming the creature's next meal upon its dreaded arrival! They had to act now.

"Finney, wake up!"

"Huh? What?"

"Come on, get yourself up!"

Finney shook his head, trying to bring himself out of his deep sleep. "Jack, why did you have to go and wake me up for? I was dreaming I was back in my own feather bed." Finney rubbed his arms to get the warm blood circulating. He could barely lift either now that a severe stiffness from the day's labor had set in. He too shivered in the unusually cold midnight air.

"Because you're not in your feather bed, and because if we don't get out of this hole, you'll never see that feather bed again!"

"I reckon you have a point there," answered Finney, as he rose to his feet. The pain in his arms caused him to grimace as he used them to lift himself. "Okay, what's your plan?"

"Take off your belt," said Jack, as he began to thread his own out from under the loops of his britches.

"Huh?"

"Your belt, give it to me!"

"Whatever you say," said Finney, as he untied the length of rope that held his britches tightly around his waist. "Are you sure they're asleep up there?"

"Yup, they're asleep. Just give a listen." Sure enough, as the boys grew silent they could make out the unmistakable sound of the two Redlegs snoring in the distance.

"Lordy Jack, they sound like two hogs rooting in the feed box!" In the night's stillness the rather odious sound seemed to echo through the trees.

"No doubt about that," answered Jack. "I can't figure how either one of them could fall off to sleep with that noise blaring in each other's ears!"

Finney removed the rope belt from the last loop in his britches and handed it to Jack. "Here you go, Jack. What are you planning to do?"

"Simple," answered Jack, as he began gathering up the pieces of the broken ladder that lay scattered all around. "We'll just tie this ladder back together and climb out."

"But Jack, we've only got two pieces of rope. It's going to take more than that to get this ladder back together."

"I know that," answered Jack. "That's why I put aside this sharp sliver of rock." Jack pulled the piece of granite from his pocket. Sure enough, as Finney rubbed his fingers across its edge it had the feel of a sharp knife. "We'll use this rock to cut our belts in as many pieces as we need."

"Think it'll work?"

"I reckon we won't know till we try."

Quietly the boys set about the task of piecing back together the broken ladder. Luckily, when Finney fell through the opening of the hole, the ladder busted into rather large pieces, making the chore a bit easier. While Finney busied himself quietly cutting the rope belts into shorter lengths, Jack reconstructed the ladder's frame by tightly securing together the pieces with the proper knot. It reminded him of the time he, Finney, Mud Armstrong, and Squirrel Puckett decided to build a rope bridge across a rather wide expanse of Rock Creek.

"And don't be tying no granny knots," said Jack, as he and Finney exchanged smiles at the thought of their earlier attempt to engineer their way across Rock Creek without getting their boots wet.

"I'll be sure of that," answered Finney, with a quiet chuckle.

It was the type of challenge that simply could not be ignored by the adventuresome boys. Jack Kelso had shown them how to run the necessary rope and tie together the wooden planks to form such a bridge. Done properly, at least according to Jack Kelso, the bridge would be both strong enough and sturdy enough to support the four of them with little worry. Of course, unlike Squirrel Puckett, Jack Kelso knew the proper way to tie a square knot. An often-made mistake when tying such a knot is to loop one end over rather than under at a particular juncture, resulting in a granny knot. Although Squirrel unknowingly secured one end of the bridge that day with a beautiful granny, the inherent problem with such a knot is that it has very little holding strength and practically no useful purpose.

It wasn't until all four of the boys were on the bridge together and over the water when the granny knot gave way. In a moment they were hurling through the air toward the shallow creek below. With the water barely a foot high in that area of the creek, it did little to cushion their stiff landing. To make matters worse, as the boys lay stuck in the cold mud of the creek a school of crawdads decided to aggressively defend their home, and began snapping at them by the hundreds. Just the sight of it caused Jack Kelso to double over in laughter. It was bad enough that their plan had fallen victim to Squirrel's inability to tie a proper knot, but to attend Church the following Sunday morning and suffer the embarrassment of Reverend Cartwright describing the event in detail—likening the granny knot in a strange way to living a sinful life—was truly a humiliating experience.

Within a few minutes, though it felt like an hour, the boys had managed to tie together enough of the ladder to reach within a foot of the opening of the hole. Although most of the ladder's rungs were too damaged to support any weight, there were enough of the protruding stubs to provide footing to the top. Quietly the boys stood for a moment and stared at the makeshift frame they hoped would bring about their freedom.

"It doesn't look too steady," said Finney.

"As long as it gets us out of this hole, I'm not complaining," said Jack, as he positioned the ladder against the rock wall and cautiously began his ascent. It was slow moving as he fixed his eye on the full moon and inched his way from one shaky piece of the ladder to the next. The sound of creaking and cracking wood filled the night air. Jack attempted to lessen the noise by softly testing each foothold before applying his full weight. It had little impact. With each step upward the ladder swayed from side to side. Jack shifted his weight to balance the rickety frame against the rock wall. Finally, having climbed as high as the ladder would take him, Jack momentarily glanced up and over the edge into the misty darkness.

"Can you see them?" asked Finney, struggling to hold the ladder steady.

"It's too dark," answered Jack, in a loud whisper. "I can't see a thing."

"Well then you best get moving because I'm coming up right behind you!" Finney hurridly stepped onto the ladder's bottom rung to begin his climb upward.

"Wait a minute!" snapped Jack. "This ladder will only hold one of us at a time! You'll have to wait till I'm all the way out!" The weakened structure nearly gave way as Jack shifted his weight ever so slightly.

"Okay, okay," assured Finney. "But don't go running off on me now!"

"Don't worry. I'll be waiting right up..." Now there is just something about the feel of a cold flintlock barrel that makes a person freeze in his tracks. Slowly, Jack looked up to find the two Redlegs glaring in at him from atop the hole. Something told him neither of the sleepy-eyed rogues found much pleasure in having their sleep disturbed. No toothless grins were apparent.

"Jack! Why are you stopping?" asked Finney. In the darkness of the hole he had no inkling of the Redlegs' presence.

"Uh...uh..." At that moment Jack could not seem to get the words to escape his quivering lips. The wobbly ladder began to shake uncontrollably. It suddenly became difficult to maintain his balance with the Redlegs staring at him.

"I'll tell you why he's stopping," interrupted Coonrod, as he peered into the hole. "Because he knows if I pull the trigger on this here turkey shooter, he's never going to see the outside of this hole again!"

Coonrod's serious tone caused Jack to quickly climb back into the hole. He barely missed landing right on top of Finney, now frozen in place by the Redlegs' presence, as he leaped the remaining six feet. As he did the ladder collapsed like a house of cards, this time breaking into even smaller pieces. It was obvious there would be no further efforts to tie together the shattered remnants and attempt another such escape.

“Come on, Coonrod. Let me shoot them!” Levi placed his finger on the trigger of his gun with a rabid look in his eyes.

“ Levi, you IGNORAMUS!” yelled Coonrod. “How do you figure we’re going to get the rest of the gold out of that rock if we shoot these two varmints?”

“Dagnabit, Coonrod! We done got us nearly twenty bags of gold stacked down in that hole. Why do we need any more of it?”

“Why? I’ll tell you why...” Coonrod grabbed his coonskin hat and brought it down on Levi’s head with a hard swat. “BECAUSE I WANT IT! Now, unless you want to end up down in that hole with them boys, I’d suggest you keep an eye on them so they don’t get away!” Coonrod placed the muzzle of his gun under Levi’s long crooked nose. “Understand?”

“You can bet your long johns on it, Coonrod.” Levi attempted to laugh, but the feel of the gun barrel made it impossible to conjure up even the slightest of cackles.

“Well then, since you’re so sure about that, I guess I can be returning to my shuteye?”

“You surely can, Coonrod! You just go right ahead, and don’t worry about waiting for me. I figure I’ll just bed down here so I can keep a real sharp eye on these young’ns.” Levi’s nervous voice cracked as he spoke. Out of the corner of his eye he shot a piercing glance toward the boys. They were fast becoming the bane of his less than honorable existence.

Coonrod mumbled a word or two and then lowered the gun from beneath Levi's nose and turned to leave. Levi breathed a heavy sigh of relief as he quietly watched him return to his bedroll next to the glowing embers of the campfire. Not a word was spoken until he was sure Coonrod was comfortably beneath his blanket and well on his way to a deep sleep. The last thing he wanted to do was disrupt Coonrod's slumber again. He reasoned that the next time, assuming it happened again, he wouldn't be so lucky.

"Now listen here you two mud-suckers!" began Levi, being careful to keep his voice low. "You done got Coonrod blaming me for your sinning ways. Next time either of you try escaping from that hole, ol' Martha here isn't going to much care about that gold when I get you in her sights!"

The boys sat quietly while Levi lay on the ground a few feet from the hole. They could hear him complaining under his breath as he gathered together some leaves and shrubs to form a pillow. He made no effort to return to the campfire to retrieve his bedroll and risk another tongue-lashing from Coonrod. Within minutes the obnoxious sound of his loud snoring pierced the quiet night.

"What now?" asked Finney, in a quiet whisper.

"I don't reckon there's much else we can do but get some shuteye," answered Jack.

"Yeah, I reckon not. We're going to need all the strength we can muster tomorrow. Something tells me them Redlegs will be expecting us to fill these bags up even quicker than we did today!"

"There's no doubt about it," answered Jack.

Finney laid back and pushed a pile of burlap bags beneath

his head. As he did he noticed that Jack had suddenly grown quiet. “Jack?”

“Huh?”

“It was a swell idea you had about escaping.”

“It would’ve been sweller had it worked.” Jack’s hopeless tone was apparent to Finney. He sat with his back against the rock wall staring into the darkness, the remnants of the ladder now strewn all around him.

Finney hated to see Jack in such a mood. Given their present circumstances, he knew it was important for both of them to keep their spirits as high as possible. To allow themselves to be demoralized at this juncture would only add to their exhaustion once the next day’s labor began. He also knew they would have to stay focused, together with one singular purpose, if there was any hope of eventually escaping their imprisonment. It was no time for blame or bitterness.

“I reckon escaping from a hole is sort of like catching fish, Jack. Sometimes you catch the big ones, and sometimes your worm nearly dies from the boredom. The important thing is you keep trying.”

Jack just offered an appreciative smile and spoke no more. As he and Finney drifted quietly off to a much-needed sleep, only an occasional bullfrog’s croak and the continuous snoring of the Redlegs disturbed the stillness of the night.

8

BAGGING THE ORE

"Get your lazy bottoms up and get to digging!" Jack opened his eyes, disappointed to see Coonrod's scruffy face peering in at him. It was a dreadful way to wake from a dead sleep. He instantly wished he could return to the quiet calm of his dream world, carelessly walking hand in hand with Becky Rutledge through a peaceful valley of prairie grass and wildflowers; he, dressed in his Sunday best, and she in an angelic white dress with lace and pastel daisies. He struggled to maintain the splendid image, but being too afraid to close his eyes with Coonrod staring at him, it quickly faded. He wondered what Becky was doing at that present moment. Being a Sunday morning, he figured her to be sitting in one of the uncomfortable pews at church with her parents. Suddenly the idea of sitting through one of Reverend Cartwright's long-winded and fiery sermons, something that only a week earlier seemed unbearable, didn't sound like such a bad proposition after all.

"Huh...what?" Finney attempted to open his eyes. He felt certain he had just closed them a few moments earlier. The events of the previous night were now just a fog. "Jack?" he began, not aware of Coonrod and Levi's close proximity. "I'm too tired to dig out anymore of that gold. Them Redlegs will just have to wait till I get some shuteye." Finney rolled over and scooped up an armload of the soft leaves to reform his pillow. In a second he was well on his way back to the tranquil state of his dream world.

"But Finney," began Jack.

KABOOM! The lead from Coonrod's flintlock left a small crater in the dirt just inches from Finney's nose.

"Okay! Okay! I'm awake!" All in one motion Finney jumped to his feet, grabbed the pick, and promptly began whacking away at the wall of gold. Jack had to jump to avoid being struck by the swinging tool. Pieces of the rock flew like projectiles in all directions. There would be no further dreaming this day.

"That's more like it," said Coonrod, as a glob of tobacco spit descended in on the boys. "I don't reckon there's more than a day's digging left if you put your backs into it." Coonrod's comment struck Jack in a peculiar sort of way. It had a certain calculating quality to it, as if Coonrod had carefully estimated the amount of work yet to be done and made plans for when the gold was finally mined. There was little comfort to be gleaned from that thought. Being stuck in the hole instilled in the boys a sense of helplessness. The thought crossed his mind once again that perhaps the Redlegs might just leave them in the hole once the gold was all mined and the bags hoisted to the top.

"I was wondering, Mister," began Jack, as he filled one of the burlap bags with the chunks and slivers of gold that flew from Finney's pick. "After we get this gold all mined, you reckon you would be kind enough to take us upstream with you so we don't have to walk all the way back to the village? You see, our canoe kind of busted up in them rapids down yonder." Jack hoped his strategy would cause Coonrod to expose his plans.

"Busted up, did it? Lordy Levi, I'm starting to feel a bit sorry for these boys, aren't you?" Coonrod's voice dribbled with sarcasm.

"I surely am," answered Levi, as his own glob of spit descended in on the boys. "You reckon we ought to oblige them?"

"I don't know. The way I figure, if we were to take these boys in the canoe, then we'd have to leave behind some of the gold. That would be sort of defeating our purpose now wouldn't it?"

"Ah, have a heart, Coonrod," pleaded Levi, in his own sarcastic manner. "You wouldn't let these young'ns risk getting sore bunions for something as unimportant as thirty, maybe forty bags of high grade ore, would you?" Neither Jack nor Finney saw much humor in the situation as the Redlegs began to laugh. It left an uneasy feeling in the boys that their predicament wasn't soon to end.

"Sore bunions? I'd say that would be the least of their worries," said Coonrod, as the smile suddenly disappeared from his face. "Levi, if you catch either of them slacking off from this point forward, shoot them!"

As Coonrod walked away, leaving Levi to watch over the boys with his flintlock at the ready, they knew by the sound of his voice that he wasn't bluffing about the shooting part. They also realized that the once radiant wall of gold was quickly becoming no more than a dark cavity, its sparkling contents now mostly bagged and stacked on the cold ground next to them. Although neither would dare speak a word with Levi gazing in at them, it was evident by the looks on their faces that each had a similar concern; that is, what would become of them once the gold was mined? It was the same sort of look that was apparent on the boys' faces the day the village constable stopped by the schoolhouse looking for the people responsible for John Duncan's new lot of half-breed piglets.

If there was one thing John Duncan was proud of above all other possessions, it was his prized Durlock swine, purchased in St. Louis after being shipped all the way from its native Ireland. His plan was to eventually purchase a Durlock boar to begin breeding and maintaining an entire lot of the highly sought after animals. Durlocks were a rare sight on the prairie. Because of their robust constitution, their quarters thick with bacon, and their ability to withstand not only the harsh Illinois winters, but also most of the prevalent diseases on the prairie, they were quite costly and difficult to acquire.

John Duncan was not a rich man. He had saved for months to purchase the animal, and even constructed a special pen to protect it from the other boars that inhabited the village. The worst thing that could happen would be for the Durlock to become impregnated by one of the puny multi-colored boars that roamed freely about. Such an occurrence would no doubt destroy any hope of ever successfully breeding a large stock of the premium swine.

To purchase a Durlock boar with which to breed his anticipated stock, Duncan devised an ingenious plan. Rather than spend an entire year trying to save enough to make the purchase, he instead pre-sold his first expected litter of the pedigree pigs to other men around the village who had an interest in acquiring a Durlock, either to breed a stock of their own, or to transform into a hardy supply of bacon. Of course the investors did demand from Duncan a promise to repay their investments if for some reason the two animals failed to consummate his plan. In a short time the needed amount was raised and an order for one Durlock boar was placed with the import merchant in St. Louis.

The day the boar arrived in the village was a gala event. The large, muscular animal rode atop the wagon like a conquering warrior trotting in to claim his newly won territory. His loud snorting signaled to all his majestic arrival. Hopes were high as the investors proudly inspected the specimen. His hide was blacker than coal and his eyes had a piercing quality to them. One of the men even dubbed him *El Diablo*! There was little doubt that once the proud animal was released into the pen with Duncan's female Durlock, a healthy litter of the fine piglets would be bred. It was only a matter of waiting for the proper moment, when the female's biological instinct aligned in perfect harmony with the boar's anticipation, to put the two together for the blessed event to take place.

Now it seems that the more attention that is drawn to a particular object by over-zealous adults, even a 300-pound Irish Durlock, the more challenged kids are to have their way with it! It was said that John Duncan fell ill for a week when the litter was born. To his disbelief the unthinkable had happened. The investors, all of whom were quite displeased to see a pen full of scrawny multi-colored piglets running about, demanded that their investments be returned rather than patiently await another year's breeding season. With no money available to make the repayment, in the end Duncan was left with no choice but to repay his disgruntled friends with a supply of ham and bacon…from both Durlocks! And what of the piglets? As they grew and started to breed and multiply with other swine around the village, the growing number of their corrupted progeny became jokingly referred to as Duncan's Durlocks!

No one ever confessed to the devious crime—opening the Durlock's gate late one night to one of the village boars—but a sigh of relief could be heard escaping the lips of both Jack and Finney when the constable left the schoolhouse that day without some youngster's shirt collar, especially their own, held firmly in his grip!

Jack continued the painstaking task of bagging up the chunks of ore. As he did, he attempted to keep an eye on Levi above to avoid being bombarded with the repugnant tobacco juice. He noticed Finney doing the same. At that moment a bit of anger began to swell inside him. If only he could reach Levi he was certain he and Finney could take him in a grapple. Of course then they would have to face the more physically imposing Coonrod. With the prospect of escaping beginning to fade, even that seemed a course of action worth considering; that is assuming they could magically find a way out of the hole to make their stand. With the ladder now busted into even more pieces than when they began their ill-fated escape attempt, and even their belts now lying about the ground in a dozen smaller lengths, finding a way out of the hole did not seem a likely possibility at this juncture.

For the moment, with Finney vigorously attacking the wall of gold with the heavy pick, the mundane chore of bagging up the sparkling rocks lulled Jack's thoughts back to a shady riverbank below New Salem. The sound of Finney striking the rock quickly faded from his awareness as a peaceful vision of the Talisman, its magnificent red paddlewheel gently guiding it to dock near the gristmill, penetrated his thoughts. Just the thought of it caused him to smile. He could almost hear the sound of the calliope echoing its melodic voice with the minstrel's rendition of Michael Row the Boat Ashore or Paul Revere's Ride. The heavenly sound of the instrument's pipes would beckon the villagers to drop all and quickly journey to the water's edge. As he fell deeper into his fantasy he could see himself on the Captain's deck holding the great steering wheel with a steady hand and a firm conviction, carefully navigating the muddy Sangamon's many bends and sandbars. It was a dream greater than all others—to one day navigate a steamer, not only down the narrow Sangamon, but also eventually on the much larger Illinois River, and then on to the mighty Mississippi, the greatest of all rivers. He had never laid eyes on the great Mississippi, but knew well of its reputation. In his memory he collected the stories and legends that were birthed by the great waterway like most boys collect snakes! Most of what he knew about the Mississippi came either from Abe or Slicky Bill, both of whom had navigated the 800 miles from St. Louis to New Orleans more than once.

It seems that all young boys have that special place where refuge can be sought from the pains of growing up. For Jack that place was undoubtedly the river. It was like an old friend; always there, always willing to listen when he needed to talk about something troubling him, and always accepting of whatever dream he claimed as his own. The river was like a glittering road that magically led everywhere all at once. Jack would spend hours listening to Abe Lincoln tell stories about the great mountain ranges of the western territories, and how a worthy flatboat, a steady hand, and a friendly current could get a man there. For Jack the river stirred a restlessness in him, and a longing for adventure like nothing else could. Perhaps it was a product of not having a family to claim as his own, but he often fantasized about simply setting adrift one day in the lazy current and letting it take him wherever it pleased. Whether down the Mississippi to the great ocean at New Orleans, or along the wide Missouri River from St. Louis to the great western territories, the destination would be less important than the journey itself.

Another loud whack of Finney's pick brought Jack's thoughts abruptly back to the present. He kicked himself for having gotten so excited about finding the gold. Given the time of day, he considered that at that moment he could be dropping a hook for 'ol Mike rather than sitting in the hole. Even his desire to sway Becky Rutledge was beginning to wane. The only thing taking up his thoughts was getting free from the hole and trekking back to the village. He pondered their predicament. Surely the Redlegs wouldn't shoot a couple of innocent boys? Or would they? He had heard many stories about the brutal methods of this savage breed of frontiersmen. They were known to hold no honor about their methods. Lying, cheating, and gouging a skinning knife in the back of some unsuspecting soul were the tools of their trade. As he considered the possibility that he and Finney might fall victim to the Redlegs' iniquitous ways, he suddenly felt very alone in the dark hole. He tried to keep an attentive eye on Levi above, but had to quickly maneuver to avoid another glob of the repulsive tobacco spit descending in on top of them.

"If you heard Coonrod, then you already know there best be no slacking off down there!" yelled Levi. "I'd suggest you both keep your eyes on that gold so I don't have to train ol' Martha here on you!" Jack quickly shifted his eyes back to the ground in front of him. "Of course I could always just shoot you anyway, and then tell Coonrod you both were slacking off. I've got half a mind to do just that, especially after taking that rock to the side of my head one of you throwed!"

Jack stopped what he was doing. The rock? He remembered the heavy stone he had thrown into the darkness at what he thought was the black curse. Could it be?

"Of course I reckon a rock to the side of the head beats getting eaten by a mad griz," said Levi. "But don't let that get you to thinking I won't shoot you just for the fun of it!"

"Griz, you say?" asked Jack, without raising his eyes from the bottom of the hole.

"Yup! She chased me and Coonrod a good mile. If it hadn't been for that hedge tree being as easy as it was to climb in a hurry, well, she surely would have had her way with both of us!" Levi recollected his close encounter with the vicious animal. As he did, he rubbed his head in the area where the large lump was just beginning to subside. "Figured you two varmints ran in the opposite direction when you heard the commotion. It would've made my life a lot easier had she trained her paws on the both of you."

As Jack's eyes momentarily met Finney's it was obvious that both were surprised to discover that the black curse, at least in this case, was nothing more than Coonrod and Levi being chased by a mad grizzly bear! Considering this, Jack began to wonder about the curse. Was it even close to them? Was it even real? It did seem odd that they had not seen nor heard from it since arriving at their present location.

If the curse's purpose really was to protect the Indian gold—as Abe had pointed out in such dramatic style—it seemed reasonable that this would be the place where it would quietly lay in wait for any unsuspecting trespassers? There was no doubting that Abe Lincoln could spin a yarn better than most. Suddenly, Jack had the sneaking suspicion he had fallen prey to his art.

By mid-morning, with the hot sun just beginning to inch its way across the clear blue sky, the sound of Finney striking the pick against the rock wall was interrupted only by Levi's loud snoring just outside the hole. Jack wondered how he could possibly sleep with the sound of their heavy labor filling the air all around them. There was no sign of Coonrod anywhere near the hole's opening. Jack reasoned there was little chance Levi would be sleeping with Coonrod close by. He wondered where he could be? In the middle of nowhere, such as they were, the possibilities seemed rather limited. He figured him to be hunting, or possibly down at the water's edge catching their evening dinner. Wherever he happened to be, Jack decided to take advantage of his absence.

"Finney!" yelled Jack, in a loud whisper. "Stop for a second!" Finney discontinued his chore and listened for any indication that Levi had awakened. No movement was detected. It was obvious that a deep sleep had set in.

"I think he's out cold," said Finney, as he threw his pick to the ground and took a seat against the wall. He rubbed his exhausted arms to ease the sharp pain shooting through his muscles.

"Keep an ear for the other one though," cautioned Jack. "I surely don't want him catching us sitting around."

"Jack? We have to figure a plan. This gold is nearly all mined, and I don't much want to think about what they have planned for us!"

"I know," answered Jack. "Whatever it is, I'm guessing it won't be much fun."

The boys sat quietly contemplating the situation as the hot sun overhead took away the last of their mid-morning shade. Even in the midst of such hopeless circumstances Finney began to smile. He too had been giving a fair amount of consideration to the black curse since Levi's description of his close encounter with the grizzly bear.

"I reckon Abe pulled a good one on you about that supposed curse of yours?"

"I wasn't the only one who believed it," answered Jack, somewhat embarrassed. "I recollect having to run like a jackrabbit just to keep up with you!"

"Okay, I admit I was at least a smidgen scared," confessed Finney. "Anyway, too bad the curse probably isn't even real. If it were, maybe we could convince it to sneak up on them Redlegs and eat them!" It was an innocent comment, but one that sparked an idea in Jack.

"Finney, that's it!"

"Huh?"

"The curse! Don't you see, it's perfect!"

The confusion was apparent on Finney's face. "Jack, didn't we just determine the curse probably doesn't exist anywhere but in Abe Lincoln's imagination?"

"Yup, but the Redlegs don't know that."

"What does that matter for?"

"Well, just supposing the Redlegs believed it was real?"

"So what if they did? How do you figure that's going to get us out of this hole?" About that time the boys could make out the thumping sound of approaching footsteps.

"Hurry, get to work!" whispered Jack, as he quickly searched for an empty burlap bag to fill. "I'll explain it later!"

"OUCH!" Levi writhed in pain as he jumped to his feet. "Now why did you have to go and kick me in the backside, Coonrod?"

"Why? I'll tell you why. Because I didn't have my hands on a gun at the time, ELSE I WOULD'VE SHOT YOU!" The boys continued to labor away, too afraid to look up.

"I was just trying to get a little shuteye."

"A little shuteye, you say?" asked Coonrod, his nose only inches from Levi's. "Meanwhile them two young'ns are probably sitting on their lazy backsides figuring more ways to escape!"

"I suppose I should've kept a better eye on them," said Levi, as he lowered his chin shamefully toward the ground to avoid being confronted by Coonrod's piercing gaze.

"I suppose you should've! I swear, Levi. If you had half the sense the good Lord gave you, you'd still be dumber than a sack of cornmeal!"

"Ah dagnabit, Coonrod. Them young'ns have done caused more trouble than they're worth. Why don't you just let me shoot them?"

"Why? I'll tell you why. Because getting that ore out of that hole is more important than shooting young'ns right at the moment!" snapped Coonrod. "Now, I'm going down to the creek to catch some catfish so we have something to eat for supper. When I get back I best find them boys digging, and you watching over them with both eyes open!"

"You can rest assured, Coonrod. I'll keep them under my eye." Levi raised his flintlock to the ready position with a resolved look on his bearded face.

"Levi, I've never rested assured on account of you. Now unless you want to see what it's like being down in that hole looking up, I'd suggest you stay awake!"

As Coonrod wandered off, Levi turned to the boys with a scowl on his face. "See there, you done got me in trouble again! I swear, that will be your last chance! I'll just dig that gold out myself rather than put up with your scheming ways!"

The boys offered no response to Levi's complaining. As he took a seat on the hard ground next to the hole he continued to mumble on about having to keep an eye on the boys while Coonrod napped at the river's edge waiting for an unsuspecting catfish to pass by his hook. With a quick wink to Finney, Jack decided it was time to set a hook of his own. He had to take advantage of Levi's current discontent with Coonrod's bullying ways.

"Excuse me, Mister?" he began, continuing to bag the ore at a quick lick to keep Levi's attention focused away from the pace of their labor.

"What?" snapped Levi.

"You reckon I might have a minute of your time?"

Levi thought for a moment. "Well," he answered, hesitantly. "I reckon as long as you don't slack off any it won't hurt nothing. But I'm warning you, the first sign of getting lazy and I'll shoot you where you stand!"

"Now I'd call that a fair warning," said Jack.

"As fair a warning as you're going to get. Now say what it is you want to say before I change my mind."

"I was wondering," continued Jack. "You being a river traveler and all, did I figure proper when I figured a full moon for tonight?"

"You did. But why are you worried about a full moon?" Levi squinted with a distrusting look on his face. "You're not going to see it from nowhere but inside that hole anyway."

"You don't know?" asked Jack.

"Know what?" asked Levi, now getting a bit irritated.

"Why, I figured you surely knew about the black curse."

"The black what?"

"The black curse. It roams these parts when the moon's full." Jack attempted to sound offhand, as if the creature's existence was common knowledge to people in these parts.

"Now what'n tarnation is a black curse?"

"Lordy, Mister. You've never heard of the curse? Why, there ain't a more hideous creature nowhere! They say it can rip a man's beating heart clean out of his body with one swipe of its claw!"

"One swipe, huh?" Levi rubbed his fingers through his chin whiskers as he pondered the thought. "It sounds to me like you've been hearing too many of them ghost stories." His laugh caused a streak of tobacco spit to run out of his mouth and down his chin.

Jack maintained his serious demeanor. By now he

had stopped bagging the chunks of ore. "Not this one, Mister. You see, I saw the creature with my own two eyes once. He was sort of a cross between a wolf and a turkey buzzard, only twice the size of a grown man! I barely escaped with my life!" Jack lowered his head and continued in a more subdued tone. "Of course, Jimmy Dinkins wasn't so lucky." Jack put his face in his hands and let out a loud sobbing sound. Seeing the drama that was unfolding, Finney jumped into the act.

"Jack, you did your best to fight the creature off. There just wasn't much else you could've done to save Jimmy." Finney put his hand on Jack's shoulder as if to console him. From the corner of his eye he could see that Levi had suddenly become a bit more attentive. The hook was definitely being set.

"Now just why would a creature such as you describe be roaming these parts?" asked Levi.

"To keep the white man from stealing this here gold," answered Jack. Levi seemed not to notice that Jack's crying eyes were absence any tears. "You see, these parts belonged to the Kickapoo before the white man moved in and ran them out. They used this gold to make things for their spirit gods."

"Spirit gods?"

"Yup, and now? Well, it seems the spirit gods are holding quite a grudge against the white man!"

"Let me guess," answered Levi, in a skeptical tone. "The black curse?"

"You figured it!" answered Jack. "No one who ever set out to find the gold ever came back to tell about it!"

Levi looked nervously about, tightly clutching his flintlock rifle. And then, once again being overcome by his skeptical nature, he slowly shifted his gaze back to the boys. "Now wait just a dadburn minute! If that curse is as bad as you say, then how did two young'ns such as yourselves expect to get away with the gold?"

"Simple," answered Jack. "We know the magic words."

"Huh?"

"Yeah, that's it, the magic words!" interjected Finney. "The only thing known that can stop the creature in its tracks."

"Magic words, you say? Now just where might I ask do young'ns like you find magic words that can scare away a creature like you describe?"

"On the lips of a dying injun," answered Jack. "He wanted to do one good deed before he passed on, and giving us the magic words was it."

Levi stood quietly in place as if attempting to determine whether the boys were bluffing. "Ah!" he said finally, shrugging them off with a wave of his hand. "I should know better than to listen to two young'ns talk about curses. Now get on back to digging that gold before I show you ol' Martha's curse!"

As Jack took the half-filled burlap bag in hand and continued to fill it with the chunks of ore, he could see Levi out of the corner of his eye continuing to look nervously about. A covert nod to Finney signaled that the plan was under way.

9

AN UNCERTAIN FUTURE

By the time the freshly cooked catfish dropped in on top of them the boys had built up an overwhelming appetite from the day's labor. The sun was just falling out of sight beyond the horizon. Scattered about the floor of the hole were the remnants of the once sparkling wall of gold. The boys sat frozen in place, too afraid to reach for the enticing meal with the Redlegs peering in at them. As their mouths watered they could only stare helplessly at the plump fish with Levi's ever-present flintlock looming above and at the ready.

Jack loved catfish. It was one of the more plentiful commodities in the village with the river so near. Even in the dead of winter, with the prairie animals hunkered down in their winter dens, making hunting and trapping difficult, it was still easy to catch a hardy supply of catfish. On the frontier the robust fish was a delicacy, especially when rolled in cornmeal and fried in lard. No one seemed to prepare a meal of the tasty fillets better than Finney's mother, the taste of which he was now reminded of as he stared at the cooked fish laying on the ground in front of him.

"You best eat that mud belly real slow-like," said Coonrod, with a toothless sneer. "It may be your last one for a spell."

The boys wondered exactly what Coonrod meant by his comment. There was a foreboding quality about it that did not go unnoticed. A quick glance between them signaled their concern. Quietly they waited for the Redlegs to depart from the hole's opening before daring to make a move for the cooked fish. Although the Redlegs seemed sincere enough in tossing them the much-needed meal, they weren't exactly the type of characters to be trusted.

"I wonder what they're planning up there?" asked Finney, confident finally that the Redlegs were out of earshot.

"I don't know," answered Jack. He quickly reached for the catfish and attempted to tear it into two equal portions. "I don't reckon they're going to shoot us though."

"What makes you so sure?" Finney could barely get the words out with his mouth full of the tasty fillet. His belly was so empty he could feel each morsel hit bottom like a heavy rock.

"Because, why would they go to the trouble of fixing supper for us if they were going to shoot us?"

"Good point," answered Finney. "You reckon they're going to let us go?"

"Something tells me we shouldn't get our hopes up for that."

Even as over-cooked as it was, the catfish could not have tasted better to the boys. It felt like days since they had last eaten. The sharp pains in their arms and backs for the moment seemed to go unnoticed as they focused entirely on consuming the tasty fish. As they quietly ate the modest rations they gazed at the rock wall in front of them, its sparkling gold now completely mined. The question of their fate weighted heavily on their minds. An ominous feeling seemed to linger in the hole like a heavy mist.

"Finney?" began Jack, as he stared into the darkness.

"Huh?"

"You ever think about dying?" There was a heaviness apparent in his voice.

"Now what kind of question is that?" asked Finney.

"Well, have you?"

Finney threw the remnants of the catfish to a corner of the hole and settled back. "Okay, I suppose I have a time or two. I don't like giving it too much thought."

"Well, what do you reckon it's like?" Jack persisted with his inquiry.

"Oh, I don't know." Finney stared up at the stars just beginning to appear in the early evening sky and contemplated the question. "I reckon it gets all dark for a second or two, and then, well, I suppose that's when you wake up in Heaven."

"You really believe there's a Heaven, Finney?"

"All I know is the last time I didn't believe there was a Heaven, I got Reverend Cartwright's hand upside the back of my scalp!" As Finney gathered up some leaves to form a pillow he noticed that Jack had suddenly taken on a more somber mood. "Jack? If you're so sure they're not going to shoot us, then why are you worrying so much about dying?"

"I'm not really worrying about it," answered Jack. "Just giving it some thought is all."

"Well you've given it all the thought it needs!" Finney attempted to jostle Jack's thoughts back to the present situation. "Now get to thinking about getting us out of this hole."

Jack just stared quietly into the darkness, oblivious to Finney's words. "Supposing there is a Heaven, what do you reckon it's like?"

Finney began to get annoyed at Jack's inattention, but then noticed a distant sort of look in his eyes. He had seen the look before, and now reasoned that Jack's talk of Heaven perhaps had less to do with their present circumstances, and more to do with the painful memories he kept tucked away in some remote corner of his memory. For Jack, the images were still there. Certain things seemed to trigger them with little warning; smells, sounds, even certain emotions. Although he never talked much about his family, Finney always seemed to know when the memories were beginning to inch their way to the surface. Being the best friends they were, he couldn't help but feel a heavy burden for Jack each time they did.

"Well now," began Finney, in a softer tone. "I reckon Heaven is about the most wonderful place a person could ever be. Sort of like going to the river at sunrise to drop a hook for ol' Mike, only lasting forever!"

"Yeah, and maybe with a whole mess of sugar biscuits sitting right next to you!" added Jack.

"No doubting it! More than either of us could eat!"

For the moment Jack appeared content as he and Finney pondered the possibility of coming across a mess of tasty sugar biscuits in Heaven. As hungry as they now were, even after consuming the plump catfish, the image caused their mouths to water. Jack licked his parched lips as if to slurp up the last speckle of the sweet frosting.

"Jack?" asked Finney, his thoughts now returning to the present. "What was that plan you were figuring earlier; the one that had something to do with the curse?"

"Simple," answered Jack. "If Levi beds down outside the hole again tonight, we make him think the curse is coming our way."

"But how's that going to get us out of this hole?"

"Well, I'm figuring Levi will want to know them magic words we were telling him about."

"But..."

"And by the time it gets real dark and quiet out, I'm betting he'll be ready to strike a deal. He lets us out of this hole, and we tell him the magic words."

"Think it'll work?" asked Finney.

"Maybe, maybe not. But unless you can think of a better plan, I'm figuring it's worth a try." Finney nodded in agreement. It was no doubt a long shot, but at that point they very quickly were running out of options. With the gold all now mined, neither of the boys much wanted to face the uncertainty the next morning held. They had to make their move before sunrise. Both had a sense that it was now or never.

In a short time, as the moon took its place high in the sky, the boys could hear Levi spreading out his bedroll just outside the hole. As he did they could hear him mumbling some garbled complaint. The irritation is his voice was clearly evident. Even in the hot Illinois summer it was preferable to be sleeping by the warm embers of a campfire once the early morning mist crept its way across the land.

"Remember, Finney," began Jack, loud enough so Levi was sure to hear. "Don't say the magic words till you can see him eyeball to eyeball, or else it won't work!"

"What if he doesn't hear me?" asked Finney, continuing the drama.

"Then God have mercy on us!"

Suddenly it grew quiet outside the hole as Levi discontinued his mumbling and stirring about. Jack nodded his head, signaling Finney to continue. It was apparent that Levi had now quietly fixed his attention on their conversation.

"Sure wish we had a gun!"

"It wouldn't matter," said Jack, projecting his voice to the top of the hole. "A lead ball can't hurt something that doesn't have no innards! It would just make him mad is all!"

"Okay, that'll be enough of the gabbing!" The boys looked up to see Levi's form silhouetted against the bright moon. "Anymore talk of them curses and you'll be the ones who don't have no innards!" The boys waited patiently to see if their hook was set. "Besides, why would a creature like you described be afraid of words anyway; even if they were magic words?"

"I don't rightly know," answered Jack. "I just know that when the creature hears them, it makes him jump like a gigged bullfrog!"

"Hmm..." Levi's hesitation signaled to Jack that the curse was more to Levi than a passing thought to be shrugged off as childish fantasy. "Just what are them magic words anyway?" he asked, trying to sound indifferent and hide his present misgivings.

"I can't say. You see, the way it works is that once I tell someone else the magic words, then they won't work magic for me anymore. They just sort of lose their power." Levi appeared to get a bit perturbed at Jack's answer. "Well then, supposing I just shoot you dead if you don't tell me?"

"It wouldn't matter," answered Jack. "I'll be dead by the gun if I don't tell you; dead by the curse if I do!"

"Can't the other one there say the words and save

you?" asked Levi, pointing toward Finney with the muzzle of his gun.

"I'm afraid not," answered Finney, trying to forge a quick and believable response to Levi's question. "It takes two people to say the words proper."

"It does, does it?" Levi was getting angrier by the minute. He stared at the boys through his squinty eyes like a poker player measuring his opponent.

"Of course, there is a way all three of us can escape the curse," said Jack, trying to spark Levi's interest.

"Keep talking."

"Well, I reckon as long as someone who doesn't know the magic words stands behind someone who does when the creature gets near, he'll have nothing to worry about."

"That's right," added Finney. "When the creature gets near, all you have to do is let us out of this hole and we'll send him on his way." The boys held their breath, waiting for his response.

Levi pondered the idea. "Coonrod would shoot me dead if I was to let you out of that hole."

Having witnessed Coonrod's usual demeanor toward Levi, Jack decided to take a gamble. "He'll never know."

"How do you figure?"

"Because, if Coonrod don't know the magic words, I don't expect he'll be shooting anyone when the creature gets finished with him!"

"Of course, that would mean all this here gold would be yours alone," added Finney. "Me and Jack, why we would just walk on back to New Salem like we never even knew you."

"Hmm..." Levi stood quietly. The boys could tell he

was deep in thought.

"LEVI!" Coonrod's approaching voice nearly startled Levi into the hole. "Did I hear you chomping your jaws with them young'ns?"

"Just long enough to tell them I'll shoot them deader than a possum if they try anything while I get some shuteye," he answered nervously, raising his flintlock to the ready position.

Coonrod peered into the dark hole. "I'd suggest you two varmints get some shuteye yourselves. You'll be getting out of this hole tomorrow, and I don't want anyone dragging their feet!"

"Does that mean we'll be heading back to New Salem?" asked Jack.

"New Salem? Well now, I don't reckon I've ever heard of such a place," answered Coonrod, as he began to laugh in a devious way. Jack suddenly had a bad feeling that heading back upstream was not part of Coonrod's plan. "Levi," he continued. "I got me a soft bed over yonder on that clump of prairie grass, and I expect to get me a good night's sleep without having to worry about these young'ns escaping!"

"Don't you worry, Coonrod. I'll keep them under my eye."

"I know you will," he continued, his feigned smile and polite tone a bit deceiving. "Because if you don't, I'M GOING TO STRING YOU UP BY YOUR TOES FROM THAT TREE OVER YONDER AND LET THE BUZZARDS HAVE YOU!" Levi shook in his boots at Coonrod's ultimatum. The boys stared into the ground, not daring to look up. There was little doubt that any failed attempt to escape now would bring Coonrod's full wrath upon them. It was also an ominous sign that to remain in the hole any longer would only increase their odds of meeting a less than desirable end to their journey.

As Coonrod retreated to the campfire, Levi quietly stretched out next to the opening of the hole. The boys each found a spot on the cold dirt floor of the hole to lay back and quietly stare up at the stars. Nothing more was said as the moon made its way across the night sky. Sometime later Jack knew by the absence of Levi's snoring that he was still awake. At one point he thought he heard Levi quietly cock the hammer of his flintlock as a hoot owl sounded its call. It was a promising sign that perhaps Jack's plan had some hope of working.

As he lay quietly beneath the moonlit sky, Jack could not help but wonder what Coonrod had planned for the next day. Whatever it was, he had an uneasy feeling about not knowing for sure. As he glanced over at Finney he could not believe that he had actually fallen into a deep sleep under such circumstances. One thing was certain, Jack knew, as the moon reached its peak high overhead, that if they didn't escape the hole by sunrise something bad awaited them. It was a simple case of now or never. The plan had to work. If it didn't they would be left to the whims of Coonrod's devious methods. It was certainly not the type of circumstance Jack felt any strong yearning to face. His eyes grew heavy as a mist began to form.

By the time Levi's loud snoring finally startled him awake, Jack had slipped into a much-needed sleep. He had no sense of how long he had been asleep, but guessed it had been quite awhile judging by the stiffness in his body from lying on the hard ground. He rubbed his eyes, attempting to fully escape the confusion of his dream world and think clearly. He glanced over at Finney who was still sleeping heavily. It was time to put their plan into action.

"Finney!" he whispered loudly.

"Huh...what?"

"Wake up! Wake up!"

With a poke to the ribs, Finney's eyes opened. "Why did you have to go and wake me up for?"

"So we can get out of this hole, that's why." Jack picked up a large rock and threw it through the top of the hole into a clump of nearby trees.

"What did you do that for?"

"Shhh..." Jack listened for any movement outside the hole. Only the calming sound of a chirping cricket could be heard breaking the night's stillness. He tossed a second rock into the trees.

"Huh...what was that?" In a split second Levi was awake and on his feet. The boys could hear him reaching for his flintlock.

"Levi!" yelled Jack in a loud whisper. "It's the creature! Get us out of here!"

"Probably just a coyote," said Levi in a nervous voice. Finney heaved another rock through the top of the hole. The sound of it caused Levi to jump and raise his flintlock.

"Coyotes don't sound like that!" said Jack, as the rock tumbled through the brush.

"You best get us out of here while you have a chance," said Finney. "The magic words won't work if we can't see him eye to eye."

"Oh lordy!" said Levi, as another rock tumbled loudly through the bushes. "Maybe I ought to be waking Coonrod?"

"We don't have time!" answered Jack. "If you don't get us out of this hole quick-like, it's going to be too late!" The boys waited for his response. To hurry him along, Jack threw one last rock through the top of the hole.

"Okay, okay!" Levi laid down his flintlock and dropped a rope into the hole. "I'll hold it. Now get on up here before that creature makes stew of us!"

Jack grabbed the rope. "When we get to the top," he whispered quietly. "Take off running. If we get split up, meet me at first light by the fork in the river."

"I'll be there," answered Finney.

Just as Jack began to make his way to the top of the hole the rope suddenly fell in on top of him. Outside the hole the boys could hear Levi fumbling to raise and aim his gun.

"Levi! What are you doing up there?"

"Sweet mother of God!" began Levi. "I've got him in my sights!"

"You do?"

"Oh lordy! It's c-c-coming right for me!"

"It is?"

"God help us! It's the ugliest creature I ever did see!" KABOOM! As the dark form continued toward him, Levi heaved his spent flintlock in the creature's direction and leaped into the hole directly on top of the boys.

"What did you do that for?" asked Jack, picking himself off the ground, confused by the happenings.

"I shot it!" answered Levi, as he now crouched low behind the boys with a look of terror on his face. "Never even slowed it none!" Jack and Finney just looked at each other. "I reckon you best start saying them magic words!"

"But we don't know no magic words, really," said Jack, as a fear began to swell up in both he and Finney. Perhaps the curse was more than Abe's colorful storytelling?

"What! You mean we're stuck in this hole and... AGH!" The sound of a match striking against the rock at the top of the hole caused all three of them to scream loudly.

"Oh no," said Levi, as he looked up to see Coonrod's illuminated face peering in at them. A small round hole was visible in his coonskin hat just above the forehead.

"Well...well...well," began Coonrod. "Ain't you a sight for a sore eye?"

"I can explain everything, Coonrod. It was these young'ns that got me to do it."

"Levi, you IGNORAMUS! Besides about letting them young'ns escape, YOU NEARLY SHOT ME DEAD!"

"I'm terrible sorry, Coonrod."

"So am I! Sorry I didn't feed you to the catfish a long time ago!"

"I promise it won't happen again."

"Well now, I believe for once you may be right, Levi!" answered Coonrod. "Especially since you're going to be sleeping down in that hole the rest of this night!"

"But Coonrod," pleaded Levi.

"Levi, one more word out of you and I'll sell you for bear bait tomorrow with them young'ns!"

Bear bait? Jack turned toward Finney with a worrisome look on his face. They both wondered what the comment could mean. Whatever it was, it didn't sound like something to look forward to with any great amount of anticipation!

"I reckon for once you'll be able to keep them boys under your eye. I'd suggest you see to it that I don't get awakened again before morning!"

As Coonrod departed the hole Levi angrily gathered a pile of the soft burlap bags and attempted to find a comfortable sleeping position. "Dadburn kids! I should've filled both of your hides full of lead!"

"Levi?" asked Jack sheepishly, as he and Finney sat motionless.

"What!"

"What was it Coonrod was saying about bear bait?"

"That's what you two are going to become when we sell you tomorrow," snapped Levi.

"You're going to sell us?"

"Yup. Coonrod met up with a couple hunters down by the river heading west for big bear country. They're willing to pay three dollars apiece for you. And it'll be none too soon when I don't have to put up with your scheming ways no more!"

"But what's that mean, they're going to use us for bear bait?"

Levi began to laugh. "It means they're going to dip you in honey, tie you to a tree, and then shoot the bear that come to feed on you."

"Huh?" Jack and Finney froze in their place.

"Don't worry, they'll feed you good so they can keep you real fat-like," Levi said, with a devious laugh. "I expect about November when the bear hibernate, assuming they haven't shot both of you for trying to escape, they'll let you go on home. By then they should have a mighty big load of hides."

"But they can't do that!" said Finney. "What if they were to miss one of them bear?"

Levi's laugh said it all. Jack looked at Finney with panic in his eyes. At that moment there was not even a thought of escaping. They now found themselves faced with a whole new predicament. As Jack lay back on the cold earth the world around him suddenly grew still. Finney lay motionless. Whether asleep or deep in thought, he said no more. Within minutes Levi's loud snoring again disrupted the night's stillness. At that moment the boys' hopes of ever seeing New Salem again began to wane.

10

BEAR BAIT!

Jack felt a great sense of relief at finally being out of the hole, notwithstanding the fact that it was Coonrod holding the other end of the rope. Unfortunately though, with one leg tied to Finney's and at least half a dozen of the narrow but heavy burlap bags hanging from his back, his relief quickly gave way to dread. Already in severe pain from repeatedly striking the heavy iron pick against the rock wall, the load on his back now made it nearly unbearable. To worsen matters, Coonrod's plan to sell them to bear hunters offered no present hope for a quick return to New Salem. From what Jack could recollect from his conversations with frontiersmen passing through the village on their way west, big bear country meant the mostly unsettled territories of the great western mountain ranges. Jack knew there were very few large settlements west of St. Louis; mostly just small outposts used by the frontiersmen to restock their supplies. He also knew the western territories were home to the largest and most hostile of the Indian tribes. He began to consider the probability that if the bears didn't get them, the Indians likely would!

Jack had met only a few real Indians in his life. Most of what he knew about them was gleaned either from the stories Abe Lincoln told him or from an occasional reading at school. He also had befriended *Chief Joe*, a supposed Fox

Indian who lived in a cabin just outside New Salem. For the most part Chief Joe had become a pathetic remnant of the great tribal leader he was rumored to have once been. Now mostly a prisoner to the distilled spirits he concocted from fruit, sugar, and yeast, Chief Joe never much wanted to discuss the glory of days long past. It was said that when a militia was formed to drive the Fox from Central Illinois north to Canada, Chief Joe, rather than stand and fight, assisted the soldiers in return for a small tract of land and a promise of immunity from prosecution for the mostly fabricated crimes which the tribe was accused of perpetrating on the white settlers, not an unusual tactic in the army's efforts to drive the remaining Indian tribes across the Mississippi or north to Canada.

Jack tended to pity Chief Joe. To see a man once a figure of such greatness, now reduced to earning his keep by selling home-brewed spirits to those around the village unable or unwilling to pay the hefty price for real whiskey, truly pained Jack. He wanted to know the Chief in his greatness, and he hated it when the men around the village would belittle him. They had reduced his majestic title to one of folly. When he would occasionally stumble his way down the main road leading through the village, it was not uncommon to hear a group of men mock him with their rendition of an Indian war whoop. Sadly, the Chief would respond with an obligatory rain dance to feed their humor, all the while barely able to maintain his balance from the intoxicating drink.

Jack knew the men of the village meant little harm in their treatment of the Chief, but he also recognized that its effect ultimately was to strip away the one thing held most dear and treasured to a man born of the wind and the earth, such as the Chief was; his pride. To Jack, Chief Joe was what he once was; a great Indian warrior; as much a part of nature as the majestic oak trees of the prairie timber. Occasionally in a rare moment of sobriety the Chief would recognize the wonderment in Jack's eyes and tell him a story of old. It was never lasting though. Invariably the stories would fade into a quiet and distant gaze. "I'll tell you more tomorrow," he would always say with a polite smile. Jack knew that for Chief Joe tomorrow never seemed to come around quite as often as the sun and the moon. He knew the Chief would again be lost in his bottle, perhaps dancing a rain dance to validate his humiliation by striking up the laughter of the villagers.

As Jack slowly made his way with the heavy bags hanging from his back like a supply mule, he considered the type of Indians they would likely come across if they found themselves on the untamed frontier. It was not a pleasant thought. He had heard stories about how the more savage of the tribes liked to scalp white men, especially unsuspecting settlers making their way west. He suddenly found himself hoping, for their own protection, that the bear hunters were more ruthless than the Indians. How dreadful, he thought, to be in a predicament that offered such a seemingly hopeless choice.

"What about the rest of the gold?" asked Levi. Even with the heavy load tied to the boys' backs, it still left a sizable number of bags stacked next to the hole awaiting transport to the river's edge.

"Well, let's figure now," began Coonrod. "It should take no more than three trips back and forth to get all them bags down to the canoe." Just the thought of spending most of the morning laboring to haul the bags of ore in the hot sun caused the boys to grimace. Jack considered suggesting to Coonrod that the chore could be greatly expedited if he and Levi were to grab a few of the bags themselves, but the look on Coonrod's scowling face, and not to mention the Redlegs' ever-present flintlocks, convinced him to hold his tongue.

"What about them bear hunters? Aren't they expecting us early-like?' asked Levi.

"Levi? Do you think I'd hand over these young'ns before getting all of our gold down to the canoe?"

"I don't reckon."

"No siree! I told them bear hunters to meet us at the fork, but not till the sun gets high in the sky. I want that ore loaded up and hid real good before they come snooping around."

"You reckon they'd try to steal it from us?"

"Wouldn't you if they were the ones who had it?" asked Coonrod.

Levi pondered the question. "I reckon you've got a point there, Coonrod."

The boys found it difficult walking the edge of the high cliffs with their legs tied together by a three-foot length of rope. Down below they could see the violent rapids that had earlier claimed their canoe and supplies. Jack momentarily gave thought to grabbing Finney and jumping over the edge in an effort to escape, but quickly ruled it out as too deadly. The jagged rocks made a leap impossible. Even if they missed and hit the water, trying to swim such a deadly current with their legs tied together would guarantee their quick demise. Instead, they continued to labor along, their backs barely able to support the load of oar. For now they would have to wait for a more opportune time to present itself to make a break for their freedom.

With the Redlegs close behind, their flintlocks in hand and at the ready, Jack considered their predicament and the possibility of ending up in the belly of a hungry bear. In one sense it frightened him, being unsure exactly what the future held. But in another he felt a strong sense of anger. In his mind the gold was rightfully his. Having spent the last two days actually digging it from its resting place in the granite wall, he felt an even greater ownership of the ore. He had to have it! It was the key to Becky Rutledge's heart. He just didn't want to accept the fact that in a very short time the gold would be well on its way downstream in the Redlegs' canoe while he and Finney trekked their way westward to big bear country.

Wish I'd never even found this map! he thought to himself. He noticed the hopeless look in Finney's eyes and was certain his thoughts were the same. Inside his shirt he could feel the piece of buckskin still stuffed tightly against his chest. Even with the gold all mined Jack felt it necessary to keep the map hidden from the Redlegs. The thought occurred to him that perhaps there was more gold in the area. He wanted to be able to locate the spot again in the future; assuming he and Finney had a future!

"Keep moving!" yelled Levi. He poked Jack in the ribs with his flintlock and motioned him forward. "You've got an awful lot of gold yet to be hauled to be tired already." Levi smiled as he thought about the pile of burlap bags still stacked at the campsite. "Coonrod, you figure yet where we're heading with all this ore?"

"As a matter of fact I have given it a fair amount

of thought. I reckon St. Louie be a good place for a couple of rich folk like us." Coonrod puffed out his chest at the thought of his newfound fortune.

"I recollect some mighty pretty women being in St. Louie," said Levi, his toothless grin stretching from ear to ear.

"That there be," said Coonrod. "I figure first we get us some of them fancy duds—city women like fancy duds you know—then I expect they'll flock to us like catfish to a chicken gizzard!"

"Really think they will?" asked Levi, with a look of anticipation.

"Ain't no doubting it!"

Finney glanced at Jack and rolled his eyes, being careful not to let the Redlegs catch him. Somehow he doubted that fancy duds would have much of an impact. He couldn't imagine any woman being attracted to the likes of these two scoundrels. He considered, given the usual aroma that emanated from both of them, that the only thing they would attract with any success would be flies!

Within a short time they came upon a steep pathway leading down to the creek's edge. Just ahead they could see the fork leading back into the Sangamon River. It was a welcomed sight to the boys. Not only did it mean they would be able to soon get the heavy loads off their backs, but it also provided a glimpse of the route back home to New Salem. It seemed like days since they had piloted their canoe into Possum Creek. The sight of the muddy river stirred their yearning to set a course upstream and never look back.

"Levi," began Coonrod. "Get on down to the bottom in case one of these young'ns takes a spill on the way down.

I don't want any of that ore spilling into the creek." Levi slung his flintlock over his shoulder and began his descent down the steep embankment. It was slow moving as he carefully negotiated each tedious step.

"Send them on!" he yelled, after finally reaching the bottom.

"Well, what are you waiting for?" asked Coonrod, as he nudged the boys forward with the muzzle of his gun. "Get on down there. And don't be trying anything funny unless you want a backside full of buckshot!"

Jack and Finney carefully began their trek down to the river's edge. With their legs tied together and the heavy loads on their backs, the going was slow and laborious. Very few rocks were available to grab ahold of or to use for a secure footing. With each step they could feel the soft eroded ground breaking away beneath their feet. They endeavored to maneuver their steps to avoid the rope growing taut and tripping them up. One misstep and they would be tumbling out of control down the embankment.

"We have to make a run for it, Jack," whispered Finney. "Or else we're going to be bear fodder before long!"

"I know," answered Jack, taking care not to let the Redlegs see him talking. "I'm clean out of ideas though. You got any?"

"I can't say that I do."

"If we could just get our legs free from this rope, then maybe...AGH!" Jack lost his footing in the soft soil. Before he or Finney could stop their forward movement, they were both tumbling head over heal down the steep embankment. The bags of ore made the descent even worse as they pounded their heads and bodies with every twist and turn. With their legs tied together as they were, any attempt to right themselves only made the plunge worse.

"Grab the gold!" yelled Coonrod. Levi dropped his gun and positioned himself to grab the burlap bags before they tumbled into the swift current of the creek. As the boys continued their uncontrolled descent and rapidly approached the bottom of the steep embankment, Levi braced himself for the impending collision.

"Oh lordy," he said to himself, seconds before the impact.

In a few short moments it was over. Jack found himself beneath Finney and only inches from the edge of the creek. Neither of the boys moved. As Jack attempted to focus his eyes a sharp pain shot through his entire body, causing him to moan loudly. Finney did the same. Scattered about the ground were the burlap bags, none of which had found their way into the swift moving water.

"Levi!" yelled Coonrod, as he swiftly descended the steep incline. "I do believe you finally did something right!" The boys looked down to find Levi flat on his back beneath them.

"Huh...what happened?" he asked, between his muffled groans.

"You saved the gold from washing away in the current, that's what happened!"

"I did?"

"You surely did. Now get up and fetch the canoe so we can load it up and go back for some more of the gold." Levi slowly lifted himself from the ground and walked toward a small inlet a few hundred feet upstream where they had their canoe stowed. Coonrod turned toward the boys.

"While he's getting the canoe you young'ns best get to gathering up that gold."

It took little prodding from the barrel of Coonrod's gun to convince the boys to get on their feet and begin picking up the loose bags. The rope that had secured their legs together was now broken and tied only to Finney's. The boys worked to quickly gather and stack the scattered bags of ore. Coonrod now focused his attention on the river, keeping a sharp eye in case the bear hunters made an early arrival.

"Are you alright?" asked Jack, in a quiet whisper.

"I think so," answered Finney. "What now?"

"I reckon it's time to bargain." Jack stacked the last bag of gold and then turned to Coonrod. "Excuse me, sir?"

"What?" asked Coonrod, impatiently.

"I was wondering…about selling us for bear bait and all?"

"What about it?"

"Well, if I was to guarantee you say five dollars apiece for us, would you let us go home?"

"Now just where would two young'ns get that kind of money?"

"Well now," continued Jack. "Finney here, his pa is a rich man. Why, five dollars apiece would be a drop in the rain barrel to him."

"It would, would it?"

"Yup." Finney looked at Jack nervously while he bargained with Coonrod. "You could tell him you saved us from them rapids, and that you lost all your pelts when your canoe took a spill. I'm sure he'd pay you a fair price for your loss."

"Is that true?" asked Coonrod, looking at Finney.

"Uh...um...well, probably," stuttered Finney. "I mean, I reckon so!"

"You seem mighty unsure of yourself," said Coonrod, as he stared into Finney's eyes. After a moment pondering the proposition, Coonrod spit a glob of tobacco just inches from Jack's feet. "You want to know what I think? I think you're scheming, and I don't like schemers! Besides, with all this gold ore in my possession, why would I be worrying about five dollars apiece for? The only thing I want is to get both of you out of my hair as quick as I can. Now get your lazy backsides moving and get ready to load that gold in the canoe!"

"So much for bargaining," said Jack, beneath his breath.

It wasn't but a few minutes before Levi returned, floating the canoe just offshore by a long rope. The boys noticed that he was walking unusually fast.

"Coonrod!" yelled Levi. "Them bear hunters are heading this way! They'll be rounding the bend real quick-like!"

"Hurry up then and get that canoe over here!" yelled Coonrod. "And you young'ns start loading them bags! Hurry!"

The boys moved quickly, each grabbing a bag and placing it in the middle of the canoe. One thing was obvious to Jack, as even Levi and Coonrod began picking up and loading the bags; the Redlegs did not want the bear hunters to know about the gold. He figured there was likely no sense of honor among these types of men. Given the opportunity, one would no doubt rob the other with a complete lack of conviction. That thought provided little solace to Jack, given that they were being set free by one only to be held captive by the other.

No sooner had they finished loading the gold when a canoe could be seen approaching from upstream. As they paddled closer, Jack's mouth became unusually dry. Something about the bear hunters scared him clean to the bone. In many ways they looked like any of the other trappers and hunters who routinely passed through New Salem on their way downstream; buckskin clothes, unshaven faces, and a certain kind of look in their eyes. These particular hunters however each had a frightening feature that made Jack tremble in his shoes; each had an assortment of scars covering nearly his entire face! Probably from fighting bear, Jack thought to himself. No sooner had he solved the mystery when another presented itself. If the belligerent animals did such damage to the hunters, what would they surely do to him and Finney? Suddenly Jack wished he were back in the hole!

"Good morning gents," said Coonrod, as he covered the pile of burlap bags just in time with a couple deer hides.

"Morning," answered one of the hunters, bluntly. "Are they our bait?"

"They are," answered Coonrod. "A couple of fine specimens, I might add."

One of the hunters got out of the canoe and walked to where Jack and Finney stood. "Any trouble out of them?" he asked, as he closely inspected each boy. "I hate to waste good money on something I might have to shoot."

"These young'ns?" asked Coonrod, as if surprised by the inquiry. "Oh no, these are well-behaved young'ns. We've hardly heard a peep out of them!"

The hunter remained silent, quietly staring at the boys. Jack and Finney were too frightened to raise their eyes from the ground. Jack noticed that even his hands were lined with deep scars. One of his arms sported a scar running nearly its full length in the unmistakable pattern of a set of claws. "We'll take them," he said finally, as he pulled a small leather bag from his pocket and threw it to Coonrod.

"I trust it's all here?" asked Coonrod, emptying the bag's contents into his hand.

"It is. Three dollars apiece."

"Well then, friend. It was a pleasure doing business with you."

The hunter turned to the boys without answering. "You belong to me now," he said, coldly. "I can bait bear with you dead or alive! It doesn't matter much to me which one it is." As he turned to walk toward the canoe the boys stood frozen in their tracks. "Well, what are you waiting for?" he yelled, turning back toward them. "Get your backsides in that canoe!"

Jack had a strange sort of feeling as he and Finney climbed into the center of the canoe. He actually found himself sorry to be leaving the Redlegs. Compared to being tied to a tree waiting for a hungry bear to approach intent upon eating them for dinner, being stuck in the hole laboring away at the rock wall did not seem like such a bad thing. If he had his druthers he would surely take neither, but at least with the Redlegs he knew sort of what to expect. The hunters on the other hand were frightening in their silence.

As they set out from the shoreline Jack caught one last glimpse of the bulge in the center of the Redlegs' canoe. A sense of anger momentarily engulfed him. He just could not bear the thought of all that gold being wasted away by Coonrod and Levi! He envisioned the two scoundrels walking the streets of St. Louis with a woman on each arm and a bottle of Tennessee whiskey in hand, both laughing and carrying on with no thought of he and Finney being tied to a tree in some wilderness location. And then a vision of Becky Rutledge presented itself. The proximity of the two conflicting thoughts only intensified his anger.

As the hunters waded close to the shore pushing the canoe against the strong current back upstream toward the muddy Sangamon, Jack and Finney looked at each other with a worried look in their eyes. Any blame for their predicament had long faded. Their only desire now was to avoid becoming bear food, and to find the quickest route back to New Salem. Unfortunately though, present circumstances as they were, their hopes for a quick return home continued to fade. For now they had little choice but to just sit quietly in the canoe and watch the Redlegs disappear out of sight behind them.

11

A NEW PREDICAMENT

The current was typically slow as the bear hunters paddled their canoe downstream. It had been a good hour since they left the inlet of Possum Creek to set a course westward on the Sangamon. The river now widened. Even given their dire circumstances, Jack still felt a tinge of excitement at venturing further west. It seemed to be every boy's dream to head toward the setting sun. For some it was the lure of gold, rumored to plentiful throughout the west, which compelled them to leave everything behind and journey toward the mountains and beyond. For others it was the lure of hunting grounds that were said to be populated with roaming herds of buffalo and dear as far as the eye could see. And for still others, those who sought solitude in a hermit's existence, the western territories offered one the opportunity to stake claim in areas where no humans had ever been, and where very few, if any, would ever pass through.

The boys sat quietly in the middle of the canoe staring at the back of the burly man in front of them. Scattered about the long vessel were all the tools of a frontiersman's trade; traps, rope, an assortment of knives and other tools, and even a small keg of gunpowder. They also had a thick stack of animal pelts. Jack tried to discern what types of animals had offered up their hides. He could make out black bear, wolf, a few coyotes, and even a lynx. They were obviously serious hunters. That thought did not put Jack's mind at much ease. He knew they would go to any length to track down and dispatch the object of their hunt, even employing the unthinkable method of using young boys such as he and Finney as their bait. He also surmised that these particular hunters settled for nothing less than the largest of the grizzly bears to feed their livelihood; those found in the foothills of the great Rocky Mountains of the Colorado territories. Such hides were highly sought after for making coats, blankets, and even boots. One large-sized grizzly could also provide enough dried jerky to feed an entire family for an entire winter.

As they headed west, Jack again considered the possibility of coming face to face with hostile Indians. Beneath the stack of pelts he noticed a supply of tobacco and whiskey. He reasoned that these items were meant mostly to be used as bargaining chips for protection and to insure safe passage through the Indian territories. Most trappers and hunters who routinely passed through these regions knew how to barter with the Indian tribes. There was a great demand among the Indians for the white man's goods, especially tobacco and spirits. They went to great lengths to protect the frontiersmen who returned each season with a fresh supply of the luxuries. Unlike the white settlers who threatened the very existence of the Indian way of life with their encroaching presence, and upon whom the tribes quickly and brutally dispensed their wrath, there seemed to be an unspoken rule to safeguard the frontiersmen's safe passage. Of course, Jack also knew there were often reports of renegade bands of Indians who were less concerned with the white man's poison, and more with preventing by any means any white man from invading or passing through their lands. No one was safe from these roving bands of warriors, their faces often painted to invoke the mystical powers of their gods and their dead forefathers. If a white man found himself in the unfortunate position of happening onto such a group, it was either kill or be killed. They seldom took prisoners.

After finally gathering up enough courage to look around, Jack turned slightly to the man paddling from the rear of the canoe. From such a short distance he was even uglier than originally thought. At first glance it shocked him so that he froze in his seat. The man's sun-baked face had deep scars etched in every direction. His eyes lay hidden beneath a thick brow, their color indiscernible behind his barely opened eyelids. Jack noticed that two of his fingers on his left hand were missing. Probably an appetizer for a hungry grizzly, he concluded. It was not a reassuring thought given their own purpose for being in the canoe heading westward.

"You hungry?" asked the hunter, as he noticed Jack looking around. It was a question neither boy had heard since leaving New Salem. Coming from this particular man, Jack became a bit confused.

"Sort of," he answered, sheepishly.

The hunter pulled his oar from the water and handed the boys a healthy portion of buffalo jerky. "Here, fill your gizzards. If you want more, it's here in the bag." The man laid the jerky near the boys and returned his oar to the lazy current.

A slight smile came across Jack's face as he and Finney busied themselves scarfing down the dried meat. Perhaps the hunters were not as bad as they originally had figured. Jack began to relax his tense body as he chewed the jerky. Finney too breathed a sigh of relief. Jack wondered if perhaps they might even become friends with the hunters. Surely then they would let them return home, and maybe even agree to take them there in the canoe. Jack decided it was worth a try to warm up to the men.

"That was nice of you giving us this jerky," he began. There was no reaction. The hunter just continued stroking his oar in the current and staring at the river ahead. "We haven't had much to eat the last couple days." Still no reaction. "Of course, them Redlegs, they weren't as courteous as you gentlemen! Yesiree, this is some mighty tasty jerky indeed."

"Glad you like it," said the hunter, without shifting his gaze away from the river. "Because griz, they don't much like skinny young'ns." Jack started to laugh at the hunter's sense of humor but quickly noticed he wasn't smiling. Suddenly a lump formed in his throat as his mouth went dry. Neither of the boys now felt much like eating the salty jerky. Jack quietly reached his hand over the edge of the canoe and let his drop into the muddy water. So much for befriending their captors, he thought. Their seemingly considerate offering was only an attempt to make them more appealing to a hungry bear.

"I don't reckon we could talk you into finding someone else to use for bait?" asked Finney. He decided at that point anything was worth a try to find a way out of their predicament. He wondered if the hunters had even a speck of kindness in their hearts. "You see, Jack and me, we want to get on home real bad-like."

"You reckoned right," answered the hunter, coldly. "Young'ns aren't so easy to come by. It's been months since the last one."

"The last one?" asked Jack, hesitantly.

The hunter began to snicker. "Yup. Jeremiah there, he found out it's not easy taking proper aim with a belly full of corn whiskey. He missed that bear by a good three foot!"

"You're a dadburn liar!" yelled the hunter paddling from the front of the canoe. "I grazed him sure enough. It wasn't my fault the wind was blowing like it was! Otherwise I would've hit him square!"

As the hunter in back continued to laugh in a devious way, Jack dearly hoped their dialogue was a practical joke. Something told him it wasn't. There was no further conversation to be had. Finney attempted another bite of the jerky but his hunger seemed to elude him. He stuffed what was left of the piece of dried meat in his shirt pocket for a future meal.

As the canoe made its way in the slow current, Jack's thoughts turned to the Redlegs. A strong anger swelled up inside him as he pictured Coonrod and Levi paddling toward Saint Louis with a canoe full of gold ore that was rightfully his and Finney's! He again pictured them trotting down a city street in their fancy new duds with a pretty woman—one no doubt in search of the fancies a couple bags of gold ore could buy—on each of their arms. How could he have been so stupid to let the Redlegs follow them right to the gold? He should have paid more attention. Just the thought of all the things he could have done with the precious ore made him fighting mad that it was now floating somewhere down the river in the Redlegs' canoe. He figured that if they ever did get back to New Salem, which at this point seemed unsure, there would be little chance of ever courting Becky Rutledge now that his fortune was lost. 'Might just as well be bear bait,' he thought, with a hopelessly sigh.

In another hour the boys noticed the river beginning to widen even more. Jack remembered from the charts Abe Lincoln had taught him to read that eventually the Sangamon made its way into the much larger Illinois River, which eventually spilled into the great Mississippi just above St. Louis. Jack had an uneasy feeling that if they were still in the canoe when it entered the Illinois their chances of seeing New Salem anytime soon, if ever, would be greatly diminished. As he hopelessly gazed at the river in front of him something suddenly caught his attention. Up ahead, and slightly off to one side of the canoe, was a large beaver dam! Immediately an idea was hatched, but they had to act quickly or else lose a golden opportunity. Before he could even signal Finney, it was obvious by the look in his eye that he too had spotted the dam, and the very same thought had entered his mind.

Now, good friends seem to have a way of knowing exactly what each other is thinking. As they approached the dam, Jack quietly lowered his hand to make sure that the rope holding together their legs, which had been retied by the hunters when they got into the canoe, was not tangled in the canoe's cargo. Finney knew exactly what to do and prepared to jump at Jack's signal. Jack took note of where the hunters' guns were sitting in the canoe and tried to figure in his head how quickly they could get to them to fire off a volley of lead in their direction. With the guns sitting just inches from the hunters' grasp, Jack knew that once in the water they would have to stay submerged until safely inside the dam. As Finney too turned slightly to gaze at the gun behind him, Jack signaled his plan by quietly pretending to take a deep breath. Finney's slight nod signaled back his understanding.

As the canoe came to within thirty feet of the beaver dam, Jack held out his closed hand just enough so that Finney could catch a glimpse of his fingers. He could hear his heart pounding as he slowly raised one finger...then two... and finally three!

"NOW," he yelled! In a second the boys were over the edge and under the water, both frantically attempting to swim with their legs tied together by the length of rope. Jack heard a muffled crack, and then felt something pass swiftly through the water past him. Moments later a second crack broke the silence. With Finney continuing to swim alongside him, Jack surmised that the second shot too had missed its mark. It was nearly impossible to see in the murky river water, but within a minute, as Jack's breath began to grow short, he could feel in front of him the tangled branches and sticks of the beaver dam. He located the dam's opening and began to surface, hoping an angry beaver was not occupying it at the present time.

"Whew, that was close!" whispered Finney, with his first breath. Fortunately, the only critter present in the dam was a small water snake that quickly wiggled its way back into the water.

"Shhh! If they hear us we'll be catfish bait instead of bear bait." Jack quietly pulled himself from the water and peeked through the sticks. Outside he could see the hunters peering into the water, each holding his gun at the ready.

"We must have hit them, Jeremiah. No young'n can stay under the water that long."

"I reckon you're right. Dadburn kids! We're six dollars poorer than when we started, and we still have no bait!"

"I guess we should've known better, Jeremiah. Young'ns are more trouble than they're worth. Let's go, we'll buy us some more when we get to St. Charles."

"We're not buying anything! We done spent all the coin we're going spend on young'ns! We'll just steal us some!"

"Well, I don't expect the griz will much care how we came about owning them. It's a shame though, them two young'ns were perfect!"

The hunters lowered their guns and returned their oars to the water. As they paddled out of earshot, Jack felt an overwhelming sense of relief. With the hunters peering back in their direction every few seconds, the boys remained perfectly still inside the tangled sticks and branches.

"Finney! They're just about out of sight!" Finney pulled himself from the water and watched as the hunters disappeared around the next bend. It was truly a welcomed sight.

"First thing's first," said Finney, as he began to untie the rope from around his leg. It took a few minutes but soon the boys were free and swimming toward the nearest riverbank. "I can already smell dinner cooking," he said, as he climbed out of the water and onto dry ground. "I'm going to get me a belly full of my mama's fried chicken, and then I'm going to climb into my feather bed and sleep for a week!" As Finney busied himself ringing out his shirt and emptying the water from his boots, he failed to notice Jack's unusually quiet demeanor as he sat on a nearby rock staring out across the river. "Jack, how long you reckon it'll take us to get back?"

"Don't rightly know," he answered, continuing his

gaze out across the river's slow current.

"Well, what route do you reckon we should take back?"

"I suppose any will do." The dispassionate tone in his voice now caught Finney's attention.

"Jack, I hope you're not thinking what I'm thinking you're thinking?"

"Finney," began Jack, his gaze now transformed into a look of determination. "I've come too far to go home without that gold. I figure it's still rightfully ours."

"Now wait just a dadburn minute, Jack! I've been stuck in a hole, shot at, nearly starved to death, and I've come closer than a flea on a coondog's belly to being eaten by a hungry bear! The only thing I'm going to do now is set a course for home! You can come with me, or you can just sit there on that rock and wait for someone else to come along and shoot you for good this time. It doesn't matter to me!" Finney quickly gathered together his boots and shirt and began to walk away. As he did, Jack never budged from his place on the rock. "Jack, as sure as the sun is going to rise tomorrow, I'm leaving to make my way home! You best get off that rock and come on!" Again, Jack refused to move. "This is your last chance!" Seeing the situation as hopeless, and not wanting to make the long trek home by himself, Finney shrugged his shoulders and took a seat on the rock next to Jack. "Well, I hope you at least have a good plan!"

"I knew I could count on you!" said Jack, with a smile.

"You can count on me all you want. It's going to take more than that to get the gold back!" Finney labored to squeeze his feet back into the wet boots. As he did Jack quietly gazed out across the river, deep in thought. There had to be away of retrieving the gold from the thieving hands of the Redlegs. He knew they would have only one opportunity. If the Redlegs made it past them, they would never again see them or their gold.

"I got it!" he said, finally.

"What?"

"The Redlegs said they were heading for St. Louis, right?"

"I recollect them saying that, yup."

"Well, they have to get to the Illinois River to make it to St. Louis. And to get to the Illinois they have to come this way."

"So?" Finney's look of confusion was apparent.

"So, there's the plan. When they get here we'll be waiting for them!"

"Well that's just dandy, Jack. But what are we going to do when they get here? Did you happen to forget, they have guns and we don't?"

"Hmm," answered Jack. "I reckon that does create a bit of a problem for us."

"I reckon it does!" snapped Finney.

"Don't worry, I'll think of something."

Finney just shook his head and rolled his eyes. "Well, while you're thinking, I'm going to take a stroll over yonder there and kick myself for even thinking you might have a plan that will actually work!"

As Finney walked away mumbling to himself, Jack continued his gaze out across the slow moving Sangamon. There had to be some way of getting back the gold. It had become obvious to Jack while still in the hole that the Redlegs weren't the brightest of thinkers. He had to figure a way to take advantage of their shortcomings. Of course, a flintlock rifle loaded with a full charge wasn't much of a shortcoming. They definitely had to figure a way around that bit of an obstacle! The more Jack pondered the possibility of getting back the gold, the more committed he became. He remembered something Abe had once told him; that as long as a man has hope he's just a few minor details away from success! That thought reassured him. At that moment, with his hope soaring high, it was now just a matter of figuring out the minor details.

12

RECAPTURING THE GOLD

Jack ran at full speed up the riverbank toward Finney. His excitement was evident by the look on his face. “Here they come!” he yelled between breaths, waving his arms in an excited frenzy. He had been patiently perched for the last three hours a quarter mile back at the river’s last bend awaiting the Redlegs’ approach.

“About time,” answered Finney. “Could you see the gold?”

“I surely could! The canoe can barely stay afloat!” Jack held his sides, attempting to catch his breath from the sprint back to Finney’s location.

“Jack, you really think this plan of yours is going to work?”

“It’s got to!” answered Jack. “If it don’t, and if them Redlegs make it to the Illinois, well, I suppose then we can just kiss our gold goodbye forever!” Jack turned to keep a watchful eye upstream. As he did, Finney took cover behind a thicket of bushes. This would be it, their final chance to retake possession of the gold. Jack felt a strong determination to succeed. Finney on the other hand wasn’t so sure about Jack’s plan. He knew the Redlegs would not look kindly upon anyone trying to steal away their gold, especially them! He also reasoned that the flintlocks he vividly recalled them possessing were probably charged and ready in the canoe.

It was not a circumstance he much desired to face anytime soon.

Within minutes the boys could make out in the distance the canoe approaching with Coonrod and Levi on board laboring to stroke their oars through the water. With such a heavy load on board the boat was barely moving in the slow current. It appeared to be drafting so low in the water that the current was only inches from overtaking it. Jack's attention was focused on the canoe's bulging cargo, now covered and out of sight from any curious passers-by who would undoubtedly have thoughts of stealing the gold for themselves if they caught wind of its presence. There was little honor among those who frequented the river. Most would shoot a man in the back without hesitation if it meant increasing his own lot in some way. The river, especially on the frontier, was well known for harboring scoundrels, thieves, and those whose picture had likely appeared on a wanted poster in some jurisdiction. The Redlegs themselves were cut from this mold. Given the method they had employed to steal the map from the old man, they certainly knew better than most the danger of transporting a load of gold ore down the river.

As Jack continued his surveillance of the approaching canoe, he also noticed the barrels of the Redlegs' flintlocks protruding from the each side of the vessel. Something told him both were ready to be called into service at a moment's notice! "Now remember," he began. "Once they get out of the canoe, you have to keep their attention until I can get an oar in the water and push away."

"What if they keep hold of their guns? Worse yet, what if I can't get around them?" Finney nervously considered the possibility.

"Then run like a scared turkey for those trees over yonder!" Jack pointed to a thick row of hedge timber along the top of the bluff and back upstream apiece. "I'll wait for you by the fork at Possum Creek."

"What if they start shooting?" asked Finney.

"Don't worry," answered Jack, trying to calm Finney's fears. "They can't outrun you. All you have to do is stay a stone's throw ahead of them. Those flintlocks will miss their mark at that distance, especially if they've been running to catch you."

"Jack, I'm not feeling too sure about all this! And something tells me they're a bit more accurate with those flintlocks than you're expecting! Don't you have another plan…maybe one that involves us just going on home and forgetting about that gold?"

"Just trust me, Finney," answered Jack. "It'll work. It's got to!"

As the canoe floated to within a hundred yards of their location the boys took their positions and prepared to implement their plan. From his vantage point atop a small bluff overlooking the river, Finney had a clear view of the approaching Redlegs. Down below, behind a small clump of bushes, Jack waited to signal Finney into action. If the plan worked, within a short time they would be safely on their way home in the Redlegs' canoe and with the entire load of gold on board. It was a masterful idea, and with a little stroke of luck, something the boys were long overdue for, the odds of retaking their fortune were at least a dash better than poor!

"Just a little bit further!" Jack whispered to himself, continuing his gaze out across the water. All his attention was focused intently on the approaching canoe. He had to wait for just the right moment to spring the trap. As the Redlegs paddled even closer, Jack could practically hear his heart beating from the excitement of the moment. It was now or never! As they paddled to within earshot, Jack signaled Finney into action with a wave of his hand.

"Help! Help!" cried Finney, in as girlish a voice as he could muster. "Please, someone help! I've twisted my ankle!"

"Levi, did you hear that?" Coonrod pulled his oar from the water and gazed toward the bluff overlooking the river.

"Hear what?"

"Shhh...listen!"

From behind the tree, Finney could see the Redlegs focusing their attention in his direction. Jack signaled him to continue the drama. The ruse appeared to be working.

"Help! Please, someone help!" His voice cracked as he strained to maintain its feminine quality.

"Lordy, Coonrod! Sounds like a woman yelling for help!"

"I know what it sounds like!" yelled Coonrod, as he sat perfectly still, continuing to gaze toward the bluff. "If she needs help, it probably means she's all alone up there."

"It probably does mean that," said Levi, as a look of excitement lit up his face. "She sounds kind of pretty, don't you think?"

"She does have a sweetness in her voice." Coonrod removed his hat and wiped the sweat from his brow.

"Maybe we best go on up that bluff and help her?" Levi began to fidget back and forth in his seat as the excitement continued to build.

"Just hold your horses!" yelled Coonrod. He continued to stare toward the source of the girlish plea.

"Dagnabit!" said Finney to himself. The Redlegs remained still in the middle of the river. Somehow he had to not only lure them from their canoe, but he had to distract them long enough for Jack to steal the vessel and its precious cargo. He had to think of something quick. Jack anxiously waited by the river's edge to move into action.

"Please, help!" he continued, in the same high-pitched voice. "I can't move! And my dress is ripped real bad! Oh please, someone help!"

"Coonrod! Did I hear her say her dress is ripped real bad-like?"

"You surely did!" answered Coonrod, as he swiftly lowered his oar into the water and began paddling for the riverbank.

Finney continued his plea for help. It was working! The Redlegs were like two fish on a hook. Within minutes they brought the tip of their canoe ashore just a short distance from where Jack crouched low behind the nearby clump of bushes. Now Finney just had to get them away from their boat and its cargo of precious gold, and preferably without their guns in hand.

"Levi?" yelled Coonrod, as Levi jumped from the canoe in a full sprint. "Where do you think you're going?"

"Why, I was going to give that lady in need a helping hand."

"Levi, you IGNORAMUS! If we both go up there, who do you expect is going to keep an eye on all this here gold?"

"I don't know," answered Levi, sheepishly. "I figured

maybe you would keep an eye fixed to it while I go up there and do the gentleman's deed."

"Well, you figured wrong! Now get on back here! I don't want anyone stealing our gold while I'm helping that poor lady in distress!"

As Coonrod began his ascent up the bluff, leaving Levi to watch over the canoe and its cargo, Finney realized his predicament. Down below, Jack was frantically pointing toward Levi, signaling Finney to somehow lure him away also. To worsen matters, both of the Redlegs had exited the canoe with their guns in hand. It was not shaping up to be a successful endeavor.

"I've got to get him away from that canoe!" said Finney to himself, aware that Coonrod was quickly making his way toward him. If he didn't, there would be no possibility of making the plan work and stealing back the gold, not to mention escaping without a load of buckshot in their backsides! Of course, with both of the Redlegs climbing the bluff toward him, the risk of being caught in the act of carrying out their devious scheme would increase substantially. It was a risk he just had to take, and he had to do it quick-like. With Coonrod getting close, Finney knew he was at the point of no return. "Excuse me!" he yelled.

"Where are you?" asked Coonrod, from halfway up the bluff.

"Just up yonder behind the big oak tree!"

"Now don't you worry yourself none," said Coonrod, already breathing heavily from the climb. "I'm almost there!"

"Can you see her yet, Coonrod?" yelled Levi, pacing nervously back and forth. At one point he walked to within three feet of where Jack crouched low behind the bush. With his attention focused totally on the girlish voice coming from atop the bluff, there was little risk of Jack being spotted.

"Levi, shut up and keep an eye on that gold!"

Again, Jack signaled Finney to try anything to get Levi away from the canoe. Coonrod was less than a minute from reaching the top of the bluff.

"Oh, mister?" continued Finney. "You reckon that other fine gent could bring me a blanket from that canoe? All this moving around has caused me to rip my dress nearly clean off my body!"

Finney's performance was masterful as Levi's excitement became too much for him to contain. In an instant he grabbed a blanket from the canoe and set off on a dead run up the hill. He nearly knocked Coonrod from his feet as he passed him by. Seeing that he had accomplished his mission, and with Levi now only moments from reaching the top himself, Finney took off running along the ridge. Down below, Jack quietly made his move toward the canoe. This was it!

"What the devil?" Levi reached the top to find nothing but dirt and grass behind the tree. "Coonrod, there's no one here!"

"How could that be?" asked Coonrod, as he too reached the top of the hill. "I know I heard her with my own two ears right behind this tree!" Confused by the happenings, the Redlegs scanned the area atop the bluff.

"Coonrod!" yelled Levi, pointing back upstream along the ridge. "Look!" Coonrod turned just in time to catch a glimpse of Finney running into a patch of timber.

"Lordy, Levi! That looked like one of them

young'ns!" No sooner had he said it when Coonrod turned to Levi with a startled look on his face. "THE CANOE!"

Sure enough, the Redlegs turned to see Jack struggling to paddle the overloaded canoe away from the riverbank. Their shock quickly gave way to action, and instantly they were running at full speed down the hill. Being the smaller of the two, Levi was the first to reach the water's edge. He struggled to get his flintlock to the ready position.

"Get him, Levi!" yelled Coonrod. Without hesitation, Levi raised his flintlock and fired one loud shot in Jack's direction. "LEVI, NO!" screamed Coonrod. "If you hit the canoe, our gold will sink to the bottom! Jump in and swim after him!"

"But I can't swim!"

"Then you best learn real quick-like!" yelled Coonrod, as he took Levi by the seat of his pants and tossed him into the river. In a panic Levi splashed about, frantically trying to stay above water. With each splash he took in a large mouth full of the terrible tasting river water. Finally, having ventured no further than six feet from the river's edge, he was able to get his footing on the muddy bottom, and proceeded no further.

"Levi, you IGNORAMUS!" Coonrod waded into the water and attempted to swat Levi over the head with his hat but lost his footing in the slimy mud and fell head first into the water. Quickly surmising Coonrod would likely come up out of the murky river madder than a wet hen, Levi scurried to escape his wrath.

"Oh, no!" yelled Jack. As he reached the middle of the river he noticed a steady stream of water pouring into the canoe through a small round hole. He pulled his oar from the water and hurried to find something to plug it with. He attempted to wedge a piece of cowhide into the opening but it was too late. Water was gushing in quicker than he could bail it out with a small tobacco can. Within seconds, much to Jack's dismay, the canoe and all its contents were beginning their descent to the bottom of the muddy river. He swam away from the doomed vessel as quickly as possible to avoid getting caught in one of its ropes and being pulled underwater. With the weight of the gold ore aboard, the canoe disappeared beneath the river's surface with one gulp of its murky water. Jack stopped and looked back just long enough to catch a final glimpse of the precious cargo beginning its descent.

By the time Jack had struggled to reach the river's edge upstream and out of sight of the Redlegs, Finney had descended the bluff and was waiting to help pull him ashore. "What happened?" he asked. Jack was so exhausted from the grueling swim he could barely move or speak.

"They shot the canoe!" he answered, between breaths. "Next thing I knew, I was swimming." The boys looked downstream to see Coonrod chasing Levi through the knee-deep water.

"Levi, you IGNORAMUS!" they heard him yell. "If I catch you I'll feed you to the catfish!" The boys chuckled at the humorous spectacle. They also felt a tinge of delight at the thought of the Redlegs themselves now having to continue their journey on foot and without the gold! It was truly a fitting end to their fiendish scheme.

"What about the gold?" asked Finney, shifting his attention back to Jack. "Can we swim down and get it?"

"Not likely," answered Jack, with a sigh of frustration. "The canoe went down somewhere out there in the middle. I was so busy swimming I couldn't get a good fix on just where it went down. It could be anywhere out there."

"Oh well," comforted Finney, trying to lighten up the moment with a slight laugh. "We may not have the gold, but at least we've got our hides!"

"Actually, we do have a bit more than just our hides," said Jack. From beneath his waterlogged shirt he pulled one of the long, narrow burlap bags. "It may not be a lot, but I'm figuring it'll be enough to make us at least a smidgen rich. I could only grab one bag before I jumped in." It was a bittersweet moment. True, they had lost their fortune to the river's dark and murky bottom, but at least they had something to show for their labor, and not to mention the trouble they would be in once they returned home. To return to the village empty handed, with nothing at all to support their grandiose claim, would no doubt lead to a less than pleasant homecoming.

Finney just smiled. "Well Jack, I suppose a smidgen rich beats none at all. Come on, we best journey on before them Redlegs decide to come back after us. I don't know about you, but I've seen all of them I ever want to see!"

"No doubting it!" answered Jack. With all the effort he could muster he picked himself up from the muddy embankment and straightened his clothes. As he and Finney set out on their long journey home, Jack returned the bag of gold to its safe place beneath his shirt. There it rested alongside the map that began their adventure. The piece of buckskin now brought a smile to Jack's face. It seemed like so long ago when he acquired it from the old man. A certain part of him felt a strong yearning to toss it in the river to rest for all eternity on the muddy bottom next to the load of ore. For the time being though, he decided to keep it. If nothing else, it would at least serve as evidence—though admittedly weak without the bag of ore to go with it—to support their story when they returned to the village to face Mr. Clary and Finney's father. Neither of the boys was much looking forward to that inescapable circumstance.

The sun was just reaching its apex in the sky when a pleasant breeze blew across the river's surface to finally cool their sun-scorched faces. For the first time since their capture the boys took notice of their surroundings as they walked. Gazing at the high bluffs that lined the river, Jack even considered that he might like to return to this spot someday. It was the type of location that always seemed to lure Jack like a catfish to a worm. With the bear hunters and the Redlegs no longer present to taint their view of things, the area through which they were passing had a certain beauty and peacefulness about it. It was a refreshing moment. Finally they were free of their captors, and at that moment heading home never sounded better! Although he was disappointed to be returning without the entire load of ore, he decided that even one bag would be more than any other kid in the village would have in a lifetime, and certainly enough to charm Becky Rutledge with a new dress and other fine things. Although to be free and homeward bound was truly a wonderful feeling, for Jack the best was hopefully yet to come.

13

THE JOURNEY HOME

"One thing is for sure, Jack," said Finney, as they walked lazily along the river's edge. "No one will believe us when we tell them where we've been!" The boys figured they were getting close to the area where the Salt Creek spills into the Sangamon. It seemed like weeks since they had passed through this area. Most of it no longer looked familiar. It certainly had been easier passing this way in Mr. Clary's sleek canoe than their current method of travel. Already their legs were getting sore from the walk.

"I reckon it does sound a bit far-fetched," answered Jack. "Of course, we do have the gold to prove it by."

"Jack, it's a cinch you ain't never had to prove something to my pa! It's going to take that bag of gold and then some to keep from getting my hide tanned!"

Jack repositioned the bag of gold underneath his shirt to a more comfortable spot. "I don't reckon I'm none the better. Mr. Clary's going to be mighty mad about his canoe, especially us taking it without his permission and all. I'll be lucky if he doesn't move my bunk out back to the chicken coop!"

"Well now," laughed Finney. "I don't expect that would be as bad as getting your backside set ablaze by a hickory stick!"

"I'm not so sure about that. At least with the hickory

stick, once it's over it's over! Mr. Clary will probably never let me forget about his canoe!"

"What are you planning to tell him?"

"I don't reckon there's much to tell but the truth!" answered Jack. "Even if he doesn't believe it?"

"Jack, something tells me even the truth is going to get us in a whole lot of trouble!"

As the boys continued their journey upstream along the river, each quietly contemplated their present circumstances. There was little doubt that their return would be met with less fanfare than the great explorers to whom Jack compared himself at the outset of their journey. The truth was, as they lumbered along in the hot afternoon sun—dirty, more than a little bit hungry, and tired to the point of exhaustion—that neither felt much like a great explorer at the present time. They were just happy to be heading in the direction of New Salem. Even their anticipated consequences didn't seem as bad when compared to what the bear hunters had in mind for them. Jack reasoned that compared to the probability of one of the hunters missing his mark just as a hungry grizzly approached the tree to which he and Finney would likely be tied, having to work extra hard for a time at the Saloon to make up for the lost canoe wasn't such a bad proposition. Besides, Mr. Clary was a reasonable man. Perhaps he would even have a forgiving heart in light of their ordeal. That is of course assuming he believed such a grand story. Jack was well aware that one of the consequences of having a reputation such as he had was that not many adults in the village were in any hurry to believe his typically grand stories, especially when attempting to explain his way out of trouble.

As for Mr. Reeves, there was little doubt what his demeanor would be. His Prussian heritage was evident in the manner in which he ruled his household. He was strong on discipline, but a fair man who demanded the best from his children. He instructed each of his boys in the blacksmithing trade from an early age and expected a full day's work out of them when not in school. Finney didn't particularly enjoy the work, but he never had the boldness to tell his father. He knew he was an integral part of the family business. His job was usually to maintain the furnace fire. This freed his father to expend more time crafting the utensils, tools, and horseshoes that provided the family income. Like any pioneer village, New Salem depended heavily on a good blacksmith who could forge the necessary items to fix wagons, horse drawn plows, and even flintlock rifles with little or no plans from which to work. Finney's father was considered the best. Finney knew that his absence had disrupted things around the shop. Although the possibility of feeling his father's wrath seemed a risk worth taking when the prospect of gold loomed large, he now hoped that the single bag of ore would be enough to sway his father's expected anger over his unannounced absence.

"Finney?" began Jack, after a long silence. "You suppose people back home figure we're dead?"

"I don't know. I reckon we have been gone longer than we expected."

A slight smile cracked Jack's lips. "Maybe they had a send-off for us?"

"Jack!" snapped Finney. "Bite your tongue! We've got enough trouble without having to explain to the whole village how we weren't really dead when they gave us a send-off! Besides, I don't want Ma and Pa coming to no funeral of mine unless I'm there!"

"It would be kind of funny though," suggested Jack, as he continued to smile. "About the time Reverend Cartwright be sending us up to Heaven, God would be asking him where we were!"

"I'm guessing God would already know where we were! I don't reckon he's much too pleased with us about now. And I sure wouldn't want to have to explain to Reverend Cartwright why we weren't really there when he sent us up!"

Jack considered the scenario. "Yeah, I reckon not. Last time I had to explain something to Reverend Cartwright it wasn't a pleasant experience!"

"You mean the time you put that bitter root in the communion wine?" asked Finney. He laughed at his recollection of the event. Jack on the other hand found little humor in the memory.

"I don't much want to remember that one!" he answered.

It began as a bet, the type of temptation Jack had little willpower to resist. After dropping the root in the large goblet before the service began, and while Reverend Cartwright busied himself welcoming his congregants, it was then simply a matter of him and Finney sitting back and waiting for the spectacle to begin. When it did, it truly was a humorous sight! In single file each member of the congregation walked to the front and took their turn sipping from the goblet as Reverend Cartwright blessed each of them. The boys had to bite their lips to keep from laughing out loud at their reactions. Believing it to be sacrilege to spit out the wine, a number of the congregants forced themselves to swallow the substance, nearly gagging in the process. Of course, some simply didn't much care about the possibility of eternal damnation. Holding the wine in their mouths, they quickly slipped out the door, being careful not to let Reverend Cartwright see them spit the bitter liquid to the wind!

"You may not want to remember that one, Jack," laughed Finney. "But I surely never will forget the look on your face when you took that gulp of communion wine!"

Unfortunately, like most such endeavors, it took little effort for Reverend Cartwright to discover the culprit. Jack tried to explain the matter away as an accident. It didn't work. In addition to the usual wages of sin lecture, something to which Jack had become quite accustomed, Reverend Cartwright also did the unthinkable and made Jack drink what was left of the awful tasting wine! For a full three days following the incident Jack lay in bed recovering from the prank gone bad, his stomach cramping with a terrible pain from having consumed the bitter root. It was certainly a lesson learned in the worse way. And once again, Jack was reminded that to attempt to get one over on Reverend Cartwright was truly like tempting God himself. It just never seemed to work as intended.

Somewhere between the fork in the river and where the Salt Creek spills into the Sangamon, the boys turned south toward Sandridge. According to Jack's map, by taking the overland route back to New Salem they could shorten their journey by perhaps half a day. Eager to get home as quickly as possible, they departed the river's edge and set out across the sun-baked clay of an open field. For the first time, especially now losing sight of the Sangamon's muddy water, they felt safe from ever again seeing their wretched captors. The need to constantly look back over their shoulders downstream, something both had been doing since losing sight of the Redlegs, now began to fade. Unfortunately though, by leaving the river they also lost the cool shade of the thick trees lining its embankment.

"Lordy, Jack," said Finney, as he wiped the sweat from his brow. "It sure is a hot day." The sun was now high in the sky and bearing down on them with a vengeance.

"No doubtin' it!" answered Jack. "I reckon we best find us some water real soon-like. I'm getting drier than the dirt beneath my feet!" Being as close to the river as they still were, the boys reasoned there would be a fresh water source somewhere close by. One thing was true of the Sangamon River; its smooth banks were disrupted frequently on either side with a multitude of small tributaries that made their way into the river from all directions, feeding it with fresh water. Some of the creeks provided a channel for rainwater to drain from the higher elevations in the area, while still others found their origin in cold springs that carried fresh water to the river from deep within the earth. Nowhere in the region could a person walk far without coming across one or the other.

"Hey, look over yonder." Finney pointed to a nearby patch of timber. "It looks like a cabin." Sure enough, a quarter mile from where the boys stood was a small cabin situated just inside the tree line. A thin plume of smoke meandered its way out the top of the stone chimney.

"They must have a well close by," said Jack. "Come on!" The boys set out on a slow run toward the cabin. There was no movement detected either inside or outside the structure. Sure enough, as they came closer they spotted a well off to one side with a large bucket dangling from its rope. Just the sight of it seemed to intensify their thirst.

"You don't suppose they would mind, do you?" asked Finney. The boys looked around as they hesitated for a moment to catch their breath. They knew the territorial nature of people on the frontier, but with their parched throats beginning to burn like hot coals, any sense of caution was quickly abandoned.

"I'm too thirsty to be worrying about anyone minding!" answered Jack, as he lowered the bucket down the long shaft. Slowly, he began to turn back the hand crank, raising a bucket of ice-cold water to the top. "Here she comes!" With the bucket just short of the shaft's opening, the crank suddenly quit turning. "What?"

"Jack, the rope's bound up." Sure enough, the rope had wound itself to one end of the cross beam and become bound between two rocks just below the opening of the well. Jack attempted to free the rope by jiggling it back and forth, but it wouldn't budge from its resting place.

"Grab hold of the back of my britches," said Jack, as he began to climb over the edge of the well. "I think I can reach it." As Finney held on, Jack leaned nearly half his body over the edge and reached for the bucket. Just as he grabbed hold of its handle and freed it from the rocks something began to move underneath his shirt. "OH NO! THE GOLD!" As the burlap bag slipped from his shirt and began its descent to the bottom of the well, Jack reached just in time to grab and hold it precariously between two fingers. Unfortunately though, with the bag's open side facing downward, the momentum caused its leather tie to come undone and allow the sparkling contents to disappear into the dark depths of the well below. Jack could do nothing but watch the pieces of rock fall into the darkness.

Finney quickly pulled Jack back out of the well. "Jack, please tell me I'm not seeing what I'm seeing?"

Jack stood speechless with the empty burlap bag in his hand. At that moment there was no thought of his thirst. It felt as though every ounce of life in him had just fallen to the bottom of the well with the gold. A knot suddenly presented itself in the pit of his empty and growling stomach.

"If you're seeing an empty bag, then you're seeing proper," he answered slowly. The boys stood motionless, quietly staring at the empty bag in Jack's hand. All that they had hoped for from their journey was now lost, first to the murky depths of the Sangamon River, and now to the bottom of the dark well. A sense of hopelessness suddenly engulfed Jack. It was just one final stroke of bad luck in the seemingly endless succession of luckless circumstances that had beleaguered their journey. He began to wonder if perhaps a curse of another kind, the kind conjured up by Reverend Cartwright, was having its just way with them?

Still wanting to quench his intense thirst, Finney leaned over the edge of the well and raised the bucket of water the remaining way to the top. "Oh well, it wasn't a total loss," he began, as he reached in the bucket and pulled out a single, shiny gold nugget. "It must have fallen in on the way down." Finney gulped down a full ladle of the cold water.

"Yeah, I reckon," answered Jack, as he slowly sat on the ground with his tired and aching back against the stone and mortar surrounding the well. Finney handed him the ladle with a fresh supply of the much-needed water. "All the trouble we went to, and now we've got nothing to show for any of it!" He couldn't believe what had just happened. How could he have been so stupid to let it happen? Out of frustration, he slapped himself on the forehead. True, it wasn't the fortune they had dug out of rock and lost to the river in the Redlegs' canoe, but at least it would have been enough to cause a few of his dreams to be realized. Now he had nothing! At that moment he felt even lower than when he and Finney realized they were stuck in the hole and at the Redlegs' mercy. At least then, before their exhaustion and empty bellies had gotten the best of them, there still seemed a ray of hope, and at least some cause for positive thinking. Now the situation seemed less than hopeless. He again considered that perhaps God was trying to tell him something in a rather straightforward manner. Was the lost gold repayment for all of his mischievous ways? There seemed no other explanation for so much bad luck in such a short period of time.

"Jack?"

"No one's going to believe us now." Jack sat stunned, oblivious to Finney's voice.

"Oh, Jack?"

"I can't believe it. It's all gone!"

"Jack!" snapped Finney.

"Huh?"

"I'm afraid our trouble's not over yet!" Jack looked up to see Finney pointing toward the cabin.

"Oh lordy!" said Jack. Walking toward them from the direction of the cabin was an old man with a gun in his hand and a look in his eye that could have scared off a mountain lion! "He doesn't look like he's fixing to offer us any kind of hospitality!"

"Jack, I figure we best get on out of here quick-like!" said Finney, as the old man pulled back the hammer on his gun and raised it to his shoulder. In an instant they were on a dead run away from the cabin. The boys ducked as the gun sounded its report, sending a lead ball tearing through the branches around them. "Head for that hill!" yelled Finney. By the time the old man's second shot rang out the boys were safely out of range.

"Whew, that was close!" gasped Jack, leaning against a tree to catch his breath.

"I'll say!" Finney wiped the sweat from his brow. "Jack, what is going to happen to us next?"

"I don't know. We can't seem to find any good luck for nothing!"

"Oh well, at least I have this." Finney handed the shiny stone he retrieved from the bucket to Jack. "I believe this is rightfully yours."

"Don't know what good it is," said Jack, staring blankly at the stone. "It sure isn't enough to even think about buying Mr. Clary a new canoe."

"Oh well," consoled Finney. "I reckon you can always just keep it as a reminder of this crazy journey we've been on."

"I won't need any reminder of that!" answered Jack. "Come on, we best be getting on." Jack considered tossing the stone from his sight, and hopefully forever from his thoughts, but instead placed it in his pocket and quietly set out walking with Finney in a southward direction toward the village.

With the afternoon growing late, the boys decided to find a place to bed down for the night. It wasn't long before they happened upon a cool stream. The fresh tasting spring water more than satisfied their thirst. Although the stream wasn't marked on Jack's map, they figured the village to be no more than a full day's walk from where they now rested, their feet buried to the ankles in the soft and silky mud of the stream bed.

Finney noticed the downtrodden look in Jack's eyes. He knew he was feeling bad about the day's happenings. "I reckon that gold was real important to you, huh?"

"It would've been nice to have."

Finney recognized something peculiar in Jack's response. "Jack? Just what was it you were going to do with that gold anyway?"

Jack hesitated for a moment, and then with a shrug of his shoulders looked up at Finney. "Ah, what's the use of hiding it? You promise not to laugh?"

"Sure, I promise." It was the sort of guarantee a young boy jumps in to with little forethought.

"And not to tell anyone?"

"I double promise!"

"Well, you see..." Jack stuttered as his eyes turned to the ground. "Ah, dagnabit, I was going to use the gold to win over Becky Rutledge!" Finney sat quietly while Jack tossed pebbles into the stream. "You see, I haven't got the kind of luck you do with the girls. You know how I was telling you about not knowing how many hearts are carved in the courting tree with my name in them?"

"I remember," answered Finney.

"Well, I can tell you sure enough how many...NONE! I also have never kissed a girl like I said. I just figured that with the gold maybe Becky Rutledge would notice me more."

Finney looked away, and then cast his own eyes toward the ground. He knew that to be less than honest at this juncture, especially given Jack's current demeanor, would be sort of like stealing from his best friend. "Jack," he began, slowly. "There's something I have to tell you."

"What?"

"Well, it seems I sort of lied too."

"Huh?"

Finney let out a long sigh. "There ain't no doubting that I have my name carved in a whole lot of them hearts. But you see, most of them, well, I sort of carved myself without telling anyone. And as far as kissing any girls? I never have either."

"No fooling?" asked Jack, suddenly perking up.

"Yeah, no fooling."

Jack looked away, trying with all his might to hide and control his building laughter. But the urge was just too great. Suddenly, he burst into an uncontrollable cackle.

"It wasn't meant to be funny!" snapped Finney, as Jack continued to laugh. The harder Finney attempted to keep a straight face, the more he too felt the urge. Within seconds he was clutching his ribs in laughter. For the moment it was a much-needed distraction from the events of the day. As they laughed themselves to tears, the woes and troubles of their journey were for the time being forgotten. Soon the question of where they would bed down for the night was answered. As they sat beneath the cool shade of a willow tree, their tired and sore feet buried in the silky mud of the creek, both boys quickly lapsed into a much-needed sleep.

14

FOOLS FOR GOLD

Finney struggled to open his eyes just as the morning sun was creeping above the horizon. The fresh morning air caused his entire body to shiver, as he rubbed his arms to assist the circulation. His feet were covered by dried mud from the streambed. He dipped them in the cold water to wash away the hardened layer of clay.

"It's about time you woke up," said Jack, sitting against the willow tree eating berries. "Here, have some breakfast."

"How long have you been awake?" asked Finney.

"Not long. I found these over yonder a piece."

Finney sat up and took a clutch of the plump berries. His ever-present hunger was quite apparent as he rubbed his arms in an effort to warm himself.

"Jack, the first thing I'm going to do when I get home is eat me the biggest mess of my mama's cooking I can get my hands on!" The berries were less than satisfying, as Finney envisioned his mother's usual breakfast laid out before him; eggs, ham, hot biscuits smothered in milk gravy, and freshly baked cinnamon bread. The image caused his mouth to water.

"I've forgotten what real food tastes like!" said Jack, as he busied himself picking the small twig of berries clean. It wasn't the most filling breakfast, but it did seem to take the edge off his hunger for a moment. Besides, it was quick, and at that moment Jack wasn't too interested in sitting still for any long duration. His only interest was in getting home as quickly as possible. "I suppose we ought to set out," he said, as he tossed the twig to the ground. "We should be home by nightfall."

"Jack, I don't know if my feet can make it that far. I've got more blisters on them than the time Hardy Beevers bet me I couldn't walk barefoot across that pile of hot wood chips!" Finney rubbed his feet and slowly began to ease on his boots. The feel of the stiff leather caused him to grimace in pain.

"I recollect you winning that bet."

"Well, if you judge winning by who ended up with Hardy's favorite snake skull, then I suppose I did win. By any other measure, especially the condition of my feet, I'd say I ended up on the short end of that wager!"

"Come on," said Jack. "If I have to, I'll carry you on my back."

The heat was already beginning to bear down hard on the backs of their necks as the boys continued their trek south across the prairie. From the look of Jack's map, they were somewhere northwest of Sandridge. From there it would be a half-day's walk to reach Petersburg, then just a short trek the remaining two miles to New Salem. With each step the boys' longing to return to the safety and comfort of home intensified. Visions of soft beds, clean clothes, and freshly set dinner tables continued to invade their thoughts. Of course, also at the forefront of their minds was the expected wrath of Finney's father and Mr. Clary, but even that seemed less a foreboding consequence the closer they came to the village.

Within an hour of departing the creek the high river bluffs had disappeared into the seemingly endless prairie. The waste high prairie grass made walking a chore. It was thicker than a horse's mane, and no discernible pathway could be detected. It was obvious that few had passed through this spot. It was common on the frontier prairie that when someone blazed a new passageway through rough terrain they would post some sort of sign or marker pointing to the spot. The same was true for river crossings. Those heading west with wagons and livestock would look for the markers of those who came before them to locate the shallowest point for crossing. It was a common courtesy on the frontier, born out of the belief that one never knew when they themselves would need a well placed marker to get through a particularly difficult area. To those migrating west, it was believed that good deeds would beget good luck, a commodity so direly needed on such a dangerous journey. Unfortunately for the boys, no markers were apparent in this particular area, as they continued slogging through the tall grass.

It wasn't long before a sudden uneasiness overcame Jack. It was a feeling that had been building for the last few miles. He knew why. It was in these parts that he and his family had gotten caught in the deadly blizzard. He was never really sure just where Mr. Clary had found him huddled up next to a tree nearly frozen to death, but suddenly he had an eerie feeling that it was close by. He tried, as young boys often do, to keep the painful thoughts locked away in some dark corner of his mind, but at that moment their strength seemed to overpower any effort to keep them hidden away. Flashes of memory began to fill his thoughts. He remembered the prairie grass, frozen and cracking as he wandered along in the blinding snow. Even the sounds returned him to that moment. As he stopped in his tracks, lost in the stillness of his painful memories, he could almost hear the deafening howl of the wind.

"What are you stopping for?" asked Finney.

"This is where it happened," answered Jack softly, staring quietly into the distance.

"Where what happened?"

"Last time I saw my ma and pa, it was here." Jack continued his gaze out across the prairie.

At that moment Finney could feel Jack's sadness. It was the first time he had heard him actually talk about his family. He was unsure just what to say at that moment. He reasoned that nothing would be more traumatic than the horror of watching your family perish in such a way. He found it painful to imagine himself having to face such a circumstance. Suddenly, he was overwhelmed by a deep sense of loneliness that seemed to bubble to the surface from somewhere deep in his soul. He wasn't lonely for himself, but for Jack. Almost in a whisper he spoke.

"I don't reckon there's much I can say, Jack."

"You don't need to," he answered, with a reassuring smile. "You know Finney, it's not easy sometimes not having a ma or pa."

"No, I don't expect it is, Jack."

"It seems like it makes everything harder than it should be…even getting girls to notice you."

"Well, I don't reckon we need to make that any harder!" A slight laugh broke through Finney's lips as he remembered their conversation from the previous afternoon. Even at that moment it was enough to tickle Jack's humor. Neither could hold back their laughter for long. As they both doubled over in a loud cackle, the painful thoughts that had momentarily escaped their dark corner were now locked safely back in their place.

"Finney?" began Jack, as his laughter subsided.

"Huh?"

"Thanks."

"For what?"

"For being the best friend I ever did have."

Finney's laughter quieted as he noticed the change in Jack's demeanor. "Well Jack," he began. "I don't reckon there's anything better to have than a good friend." Finney spit into the palm of his hand and offered it in the customary manner. "Friends forever?"

"Friends forever!" answered Jack, as he too spit into his hand and grabbed Finney's in a firm grasp.

Nothing more was said about the subject. Though the images and memories would no doubt again find their way to the surface, for now Jack was just happy to be heading home. It was a good feeling to have a friend like Finney. He knew he could count on him as best friends do. He still felt a bit guilty though for having gotten Finney into such a predicament. He truly hoped he harbored no ill feelings.

"Finney?" he asked.

"Huh?"

"You're not mad at me are you?"

"For what?"

"For getting you in this mess. I guess it wasn't the brightest idea I've ever had."

"Naw," answered Finney. "I suppose I was wanting

that gold just as bad as you were, Jack. Besides, if I thought it was such a bad idea going to look for it, well, I don't reckon I would've gone with you."

"Yeah, I reckon not," answered Jack, with a smile. He felt relieved to know that Finney held no anger toward him, especially now that the gold had slipped from their grasp.

"The way I figure it," continued Finney. "The journey wasn't a total loss."

"How do you figure?" asked Jack.

"Well, it isn't everyday a boy gets to be captured by two varmints the likes of them Redlegs; then escape from bear hunters; and not to mention being shot at and nearly starved to death! If you want Becky Rutledge to notice you, well, just imagine how brave she's going to think you are when she hears all that!"

"Hmm..." Jack pondered the idea. "I guess I never thought of it that way. Of course, that is assuming she believes us in the first place."

"Yeah, I reckon that's going to be the hardest part for both of us!" acknowledged Finney, still giving thought to how he was going to explain the situation to his father.

By the time the sun reached its apex in the sky the boys had happened upon a wagon trail leading south. It was a promising sight. It meant that Petersburg had to be close by. Jack figured it to be less than ten miles ahead. Once there, New Salem would be just a short walk to the south. Their discovery of the worn pathway came none too soon. As Finney's blistered feet worsened, laboring through the tall prairie grass was becoming unbearable. Now on the dirt road he was able to remove his boots and walk on his bare feet. It relieved the pain from the blisters sure enough, but now he had to deal with the extreme heat of the dirt on his feet. Every few yards he had to jump off the road and onto the soft grass to bring some relief.

"Look over there," said Jack. Up ahead and just off to the side of the pathway was a wagon, next to which a single horse lazily drank from a small creek.

"Jack, I surely hope that wagon is heading south. I don't expect I can make it much further on this hot dirt. My feet are blazing!"

"I don't see anyone tending to it," said Jack.

The horse barely flinched as the boys reached the idle wagon. Finney immediately hopped onto the back and began rubbing his sore feet. "Lordy, that sure feels good! Who do you think this wagon belongs to, Jack?"

"I believe it belongs to me," came a gentle voice from just inside the tree line. The boys turned to see an old man walking from the timber. His round, bearded face lit up with a friendly sort of smile; not like the old man at the cabin. "Unusual seeing young'ns walking these parts."

"Is this your rig, mister?" asked Jack.

"It is."

"Well, my friend here, he's got blisters real bad. I was wondering if maybe you're heading in the direction of New Salem?" The boys held their breath, hoping the man was heading toward home. The thought of riding the remainder of the way on the back of the wagon appealed greatly to both of them.

"Hmm..." The old man peered over at Finney's feet. "I don't reckon I am, sorry to say. Heading west of there, toward Little Grove Creek."

Jack let out a long sigh. Being so close to home and not wanting to sit idle any longer than was necessary, he motioned for Finney to slide off the back of the wagon so they could continue their journey. Finney could barely make the short jump. As he landed on the ground his sore feet caused his legs to buckle. He tried to hide the pain, but Jack could easily discern it. Jack now began to consider the possibility of having to carry Finney on his back for a time. It was not an enjoyable thought, but he knew he had to do whatever was necessary. After all, they were best friends, and Jack knew Finney would willingly do the same for him if their circumstances were switched. Besides, neither wanted to spend another night away from home. By now their hunger was intense. Both were experiencing an uncomfortable pain in his belly, only worsened by the sour berries they consumed for breakfast.

As the boys turned slowly to depart the old man's presence, Jack suddenly remembered something! It was worth a try. He pulled the gold nugget from his pocket. "Mister, what if I was to pay you a handsome price for your trouble? Would you be willing to go out of your way a piece?"

"Jack!" whispered Finney. "That's the last one. Don't waste it on account of my feet!"

"Hush!" answered Jack, in a loud whisper.

"Well," began the old man, rubbing his chin and considering the proposition. "I reckon it would be a good piece out of my way. And Daisy here, she can hardly pull more than one person at a time."

"I can pay you in gold!"

"Gold!" The old man's face lit up. "Well now, that throw's a different light on the idea. How much are you offering?"

"Right here," answered Jack, as he proudly held open his outstretched hand. The old man took the piece of ore, tossed it up and down to measure its weight, and then placed it between his teeth and gently bit down on its surface.

"Where did you get this?" he asked, throwing the stone back to Jack.

"North of here a piece."

"Well," began the old man, as a huge smile stretched across his face. "You've got yourself one of the finest nuggets of fool's gold I ever did see!"

"Fool's what?" asked Jack.

"Fool's gold. There's lots of it up around Possum Creek."

"You mean this nugget is something different than the real kind of gold?" asked Jack, as a shocked look suddenly appeared on his face.

"Yup," continued the old man. "Fool's gold looks like real gold. Even tastes a bit like real gold. The problem is, it's worth no more than the rock you dig it from."

Jack's mouth fell open. Slowly he turned toward Finney. "I'm beginning to feel a sick kind of feeling inside."
"I know," said Finney, with a look of disbelief. "I'm feeling the same." Slowly, he began to put his boots back on his blistered feet. "Come on, Jack. I reckon we best get on."

As the boys turned to walk away, the desolation apparent on both their faces, the old man stood in place rubbing his chin. "Now just hold on, young'ns," he said. "I reckon I could get you as far as Petersburg, but not an inch further!"

"But we have nothing to pay you with, mister," said Jack.

"Well," he answered, his friendly smile again etched across his face. "That fool's gold reminded me of something from a long time ago. Let's just say I'll take the memory as payment for my trouble."

"Gee thanks, mister!" The boys quickly jumped onto the back of the wagon, thankful that they had happened upon the old man and his horse.

"The name's Grady," said the old man, as he strapped the horse back to the wagon. "Grady O'Reilly."

"My name's Jack. Back home they call me Salem Jack. And this here's Finnigan Reeves."

"Well now, Salem Jack and Finnigan Reeves, I'm mighty pleased to know you. Now tell me about that fool's gold. Something tells me you've got a mighty good story to tell!"

"Well," began Jack, as he looked across at Finney. "You ever hear tell of the black curse?"

In a few short minutes the wagon was heading south toward home with Finney rubbing his tired and blistered feet, Jack telling the story of their unbelievable journey, and the old man gently guiding the tired old horse down the worn and bumpy pathway. Left behind, and lost for all eternity in the tall prairie grass, was the nugget of fool's gold right where Jack had dropped it. All that was important now was that they were heading south toward New Salem. Within a few hours they would be in Petersburg, leaving them just a short walk of two miles back to the village. Although they would be returning with no gold in their possession, their clothes ruined beyond mending, and the canoe and everything in it lost, at that moment home sounded better than a barrel of sugar biscuits!

15

A BETTER MAN

Jack was awake and out of bed early to avoid coming face to face with Mr. Clary. After the lecture he received the night before when Mr. Clary discovered him sneaking into the saloon through the back window, especially after Jack broke the news about the canoe, instilled in him a strong desire to avoid any further contact with him until his temper calmed a bit. Even telling him about how they were kidnapped by the Redlegs seemed to have little impact on his anger. Jack couldn't tell if he even believed the story. In case he didn't, he figured it best not to mention the bear hunters. As Mr. Clary angrily reminded Jack how the saloon floor had gone unswept since his disappearance, being stuck in a hole under the watchful eyes of Coonrod and Levi suddenly seemed an attractive alternative.

"Howdy Abe," said Jack, as he walked through the open door of the Lincoln-Berry Store. The store was a place of refuge for Jack. He often came there to confer with Abe when deep in thought or troubled by any particular matter. Not only was Abe the smartest person he personally knew, with the possible exception of Jack Kelso, who busied himself reading the likes of Shakespeare and Milton when not pursuing his usual routine of dropping a hook and line in the muddy Sangamon, but Abe also seemed to understand him better than most, and always treated him with the respect due a grown man. Seldom was a problem so big that it couldn't be solved while jabbering with Abe over a game of checkers and a cup of sweet sassafras.

"Well now," said Abe. "If it isn't the lost traveler! How about a cup of tea? It just happens I have a fresh stock of some of the sweetest root I've ever tasted!"

"I suppose," answered Jack, with a downtrodden look on his face.

"I saw Finnigan Reeves' pappy this morning. He tells me Finny told quite a story about where you boys have been the past few days."

"It's not a story, Abe!" snapped Jack. "It happened just the way he said!" He wanted Abe to believe him in the worst way. He was perhaps the only person in the village who might, Jack reasoned. There was little chance anyone else would accept such a grandiose story with any amount of credence.

"Well then Jack, I suppose it did." Abe filled the tin cup to the brim with the sweet tea. "It's just sometimes adults, they don't want to believe young'ns so easy."

"I know," said Jack, in a somber tone. "I don't expect Mr. Clary will ever believe me again."

"He's not pleased with you, eh?"

"Not a bit! Especially after hearing we lost his canoe to those rapids. I'll be sweeping floors at the saloon the rest of my life to pay for it!"

Abe stood quietly, rubbing his chin. "Tell you what. You know those two old hedge trees out back?" Jack nodded his head. "What if I was to pay you say two bits for cutting them down? You reckon you'd be interested?"

"I don't reckon I have a choice." Jack took a drink

from the tin cup and then looked up at Abe. "Abe, you believe us don't you? I mean, just the way Finney told his pa?"

"Well Jack, I don't reckon I have a good reason not to believe you. Besides, if what you say is true, then it really doesn't matter what I believe or don't believe. The important thing is you're being honest, and a man who can shut his eyes at night knowing he told the truth, well let's just say he'll wake up a better man for it."

"I don't feel like a better man at the moment, Abe. I feel kind of silly for getting Finney and me in such a mess over a load of gold that wasn't even real gold!"

"Fool's gold, huh?" asked Abe.

"Yup, nearly forty bags of it. We dug it out of that rock wall while them Redlegs stood over us with their flintlocks at the ready. They nearly shot us more than once! Of course, they weren't half as bad as those bear hunters. Finney and me, we came that close to being bear bait!"

"It doesn't sound like any kind of thing to be!" said Abe, his slight smile apparent.

"I'll say! If it wasn't for that beaver dam we swam inside of, we'd be well on our way to being tied to a tree somewhere waiting for griz to come and feed on us!"

"Jack, it does sound like quite an adventure you boys had."

"I surely never want to go on another one like it!" Jack was glad Abe believed his story. Even if he was only pretending, something Jack failed to discern, he appreciated Abe's demeanor toward him. He knew Abe would likely be the only one in the village who would even consider such a far-fetched tale, especially coming from a couple of boys who were well known for spinning yarns on a grand scale.

It was obvious Mr. Clary wasn't going to believe them. Jack took a final drink from his cup. "I'll be by this afternoon to start cutting on them hedge trees, Abe."

"I'll be expecting you," answered Abe, as Jack turned to leave the store. "Oh, and Jack?"

"Huh?"

"Take this." Abe tossed a shiny nickel through the air. "We'll call that an advance on the two bits I'll be owing you."

"But why are you giving it to me now?" asked Jack.

"Remember what I was saying about waking up a better man?" began Abe. "Well, sometimes a stroke of good luck comes with it. Let's just say I have a feeling you'll be needing it."

"Thanks Abe," said Jack, as he placed the nickel in his pocket. "I reckon a stroke of good luck is just what I need about now."

The short trek through the village and down to the river's edge was a quiet one. Being a Sunday morning, most of the villagers were packed into the church listening to one of Reverend Cartwright's fire and brimstone sermons. Jack wanted to avoid Reverend Cartwright at all costs lest he wanted to sit through another of his lectures on the virtues of honesty. With Finney's father being a church elder, Jack figured at that moment Finney was no doubt being held captive to the front pew and feeling the full force of Reverend Cartwright's passionate delivery. It was definitely no place for a young boy in their situation to be!

Even the river itself was unusually quiet as Jack took a seat on his favorite rock and began tossing stones across the water's still surface. "You out there, ol' Mike?" Jack took the buckskin map from underneath his shirt. "Can you believe it? All the trouble we went through for a hole full of worthless rock! I swear ol' Mike, sometimes I just have no luck at all!" Just as Jack prepared to toss the map into the slow moving current he was startled by an approaching voice.

"Jack, I've been looking all over for you." Jack turned to see Finney approaching from atop the bluff.

"I figured you were in Church," said Jack.

"It just let out. I took off real quick-like before Reverend Cartwright got hold of me!"

"Yeah, I don't reckon he believes us either."

"Why should he?" laughed Finney. "No one else in the village seems to. Hey, what are you doing down here?"

"I'm trying to figure a way to pay for Mr. Clary's canoe!" Jack tossed another rock across the water.

"Well, that makes two of us. My pa says I have to pay for half of it."

"Gee, that's just great," answered Jack. "It means I'll only have to sweep floors for just half the rest of my life instead of all of it!"

"Ah, it's not so bad, Jack. Why, it sure beats being tied to a tree somewhere waiting for griz to come and feed on us!"

"Depends on how you look at it," said Jack, dejectedly. He just knew that without the gold there was little hope of ever courting Becky Rutledge. There was little doubt she would disbelieve their far-fetched tale and think less of the both of them. Jack reasoned that she would likely never again even talk to him in a serious way. What could be worse? The self-confidence that seemed to soar at the outset of their journey now seemed to quietly fade into oblivion.

"Well, one thing's for sure," said Finney, as he painfully sat on the rock next to Jack. "I'm never again going to mention Redlegs, black curses, or gold to anyone! My pa done cut a new hickory stick to replace the one he broke over my backside last night. I don't reckon I much want to break another."

About that time, as the church bell sounded its call off in the distance, the boys turned to see Sally Armstrong and Becky Rutledge walking in their direction from atop the bluff.

"Great!" said Jack, hopelessly. "They're probably coming to laugh at us!"

"Finnigan Reeves," said Sally, as they reached the rock where the boys sat. Both of them stared into the ground to hide their sudden embarrassment. "I looked for you after Church. You took off before I could catch you."

"You were looking for me?" asked Finney, the disbelief apparent in his voice.

"I surely was. My pa says I can invite you over for a Sunday picnic if you like. My mother fixing fried chicken."

"Why sure!" blurted Finney, suddenly perking up. "I'd love to!"

"Figures!" mumbled Jack, to himself.

"Jack, I'll be seeing you around," said Finney, his attention now focused on Sally Armstrong's outstretched hand.

"Sure," answered Jack, quite detached from the happenings. As Finney and Sally walked hand in hand toward the bluff, he quietly continued his gaze out across the river.

" That's quite a story you and Finney are telling about

where you've been," began Becky, still standing in place next to the rock. "The whole congregation was talking about it."

"Yeah, well it isn't a story!" snapped Jack, as he held out the map for Becky to see. "Right here's the map!"

"Jack," continued Becky, without even looking at the piece of buckskin. "Sometimes I just can't figure you out. You're so busy dreaming about steamboats and gold, why I can't get you to take an interest in me for nothing!"

"Yeah, well just maybe..." Jack's voice stopped dead in its tracks. "You mind repeating that?"

Becky looked at the ground as her cheeks turned a blush red. "I was saying how I've wanted you to notice me."

"You have?" Jack shook his head as if to clear his ears.

"Yup. Of course, if you're too busy looking for gold..."

"Gold?" asked Jack, as he quickly pulled the map behind his back. "What gold?"

"Jack? You suppose you might have an interest in buying me a licorice stick up at Abe's?"

"Uh...well..." began Jack, with a bit of hesitation. Just as he lowered his head, preparing to inform Becky of his usual lack of money, he remembered the nickel advance Abe had given him. "Sure!" he blurted out with excitement. "I'd like that!"

Becky held out her hand. "Then I reckon we best be moving along, don't you think?"

"Yeah, I reckon so," answered Jack, still somewhat overwhelmed by the happenings. He couldn't believe it! The girl of his dreams wanting him to take notice of her! Was this actually happening? The softness of her hand was like the fragile petals of a wildflower. As the two walked toward the bluff, Jack recalled his conversation with Abe Lincoln. "I reckon Abe was right," he mumbled, half under his breath.

"What was that?" asked Becky.

"Oh, nothing really," he answered, with a smile. "Just something Abe Lincoln was saying about waking up a better man..."

As the two disappeared into the trees, slowly making its way downstream in the muddy current was the buckskin map. At that moment in time, especially for a young boy named Salem Jack, gold had suddenly slipped into the realm of lesser important things....

The End

www.ingramcontent.com/pod-product-compliance
Lightning Source LLC
Chambersburg PA
CBHW070608310726
48982CB00001B/17

* 9 7 8 0 5 7 8 2 8 2 8 8 6 *